For Alana, with much love . . . T.C.

Chapter 1

Blueberry Muffin was cross. Bryony could always tell. He was perched, rather stiffly, on the end of her bed, staring ahead at thin air.

'Sorry, Berry,' Bryony said. 'When it stops raining you'll feel better. Then we'll go and explore together. We'll *love* Brook Dale, you'll see!'

She stroked her cat's silvery fur but he flatly refused to purr, so she strolled across the bare floorboards to her window instead.

Bryony rubbed the misted-up glass and peered down the garden to what looked like plum trees. This must have been how Plum Cottage had got its name, she thought. Last night they'd arrived too

late to see anything much, but now she saw the garden looked rambling and wild.

'Ahhh . . .' Bryony suddenly heard herself sigh. Wandering back to her bed, she sat down close to Berry. He wasn't the only one feeling out of place . . .

She gazed around her new bedroom crammed with unpacked boxes. It was small and the walls were thick and lopsided. It had someone else's smell, someone else's wallpaper. It looked nothing like her old bedroom she'd left behind.

'It'll be okay,' said her grown-up voice inside, '. . . you only arrived last night. Things are *bound* to feel different. Give it time.'

With a faint *meow*, Berry rolled onto his back and presented his tummy to be tickled. Maybe he was coming round a bit.

'Grandpa's visiting later,' Bryony said, stroking the cat's warm, round tummy. 'He might even bring you some fish if you're lucky, eh?'

Bryony surprised herself now with a smile, which must have come from thinking of her grandfather. Albert Wallace had a warm smile too, and he was really kind. Grandpa, like Bryony,

loved to be busy, with new projects always on the go. Now Bryony would be able to see him much more than ever she could before. In fact, one of the reasons they'd moved to Brook Dale was to be closer to him. That, and to make a 'fresh start' in this run-down old cottage by the sea.

Bryony pulled across a packing box and started to rummage inside. An assortment of objects steadily littered her quilt as she delved deeper into its depths. A book on gemstones, a handful of pens, some hair ties and several odd socks. Then, finally, she fished out *just* the thing.

'There!' said Bryony, clutching the picture frame. She licked her finger and rubbed a smudge off the glass. 'Welcome to rainy Brook Dale, everyone!'

Bryony thought of her two best friends standing beside her in the photo. She wondered what they'd both be up to now. Becky – small, blonde and freckly, and tall, skinny Fran with black hair. And there in the middle was Bryony, her wild auburn hair forced into plaits and her sea-green eyes smiling. Bryony was at her happiest when surrounded by friends.

She poked around in the box again and pulled out a big red rosette. The same one she was wearing in the photo. *Park Lodge Stables – First Prize*, it said. She'd won it at her riding school's gymkhana last year. As she smoothed the crumpled ribbons flat, she recalled that special day . . .

Right at the start of the morning, everyone had drawn straws to decide which pony they'd ride. Poor Fran had ended up with Boris-the-Bold who wasn't very bold at all (unless you counted nibbling the judge's jumper!). Becky had had more luck on jet-black Midnight, coming second in the Barrel Race. But Peppermint, the pony that Bryony had drawn, had been the *real* star that day. A cool calm grey with flecks of silver, Peppermint reminded Bryony of a unicorn. And that day she had jumped so smoothly it had felt to Bryony like they were actually flying!

The next photo out of the box was one of the family, taken on holiday in France a few years ago. She and her twin brother, Josh, were in the centre. Josh, who was younger than Bryony by seven minutes, was slightly taller than her, and his scruffy hair was brown and much straighter. Beside Josh was Mum, and beside Bryony (with the same curly hair and green eyes as she had) was . . .

'*Dad*.' Bryony whispered the word, which ended in a hushed deep sigh.

It had only been six months since he'd died and she missed him *so much*. And now moving house somehow made it feel even longer since they were all together as a family.

A tear escaped from Bryony's eye before she could dab it away. She quickly hugged the photo close to her chest, like if Dad saw her crying it would make *him* sad too. Silly, she knew. But it was just how she felt. Dad had always said how proud he was of the way she smiled and got on with things. She mopped up the tear with the cuff of her sleeve. She *wouldn't* let Dad down, whatever . . .

'Right then!' said her grown-up voice inside. 'Just think of moving as an adventure. You really like adventures, you know you do!'

Bryony nodded. That was true. She'd never been scared of adventures. In fact, she'd always *loved* the feeling of butterflies in her tummy. That wonderful, tingly feeling she'd got the first time she ever sat on a pony. Or when she'd first trotted,

or cantered, or galloped, or attempted her very first jump!

She put both photos on her bedside table. These memories would always be with her, like Dad would – wherever she was. And now she was here, it was the summer holidays and time for her to get out and make even *more* memories ...

*

A spring in her mattress gave a small twang as Bryony got off her bed. Berry opened one eye to show his annoyance.

'Time for breakfast,' Bryony said with a yawn. The cat's eye shut again. 'Okay,' she shrugged. 'See you later then.'

She opened the door and headed out, the floorboards creaking noisily. Those would need sorting. This cottage was falling to bits!

A long queue of packing boxes lined the landing wall. They looked almost bored, like they were waiting for a very late bus.

'I'll be back!' Bryony told them, as if they could understand. Straight after breakfast, she promised herself, she'd start on the unpacking. *This* was

home now and the sooner she made it feel like that the better.

At the bottom of the steep, dark staircase, the warm smell of toast filled the air. 'Just what I need,' Bryony said. Mum always had a knack of knowing.

She closed her eyes to breathe in the smell when suddenly a torrent of eager footsteps sounded on the stairs behind.

'Out the way!' yelled Josh impatiently, jumping the last four steps. 'Smells like things are looking up! *Toast time*.'

She saw the back of her twin brother's head disappear through the kitchen doorway. 'Hey – save some for *me*!' called Bryony, hurrying after him.

The kitchen was already Bryony's favourite room. She'd decided that last night. It felt familiar, comfy – worn in, like her favourite pair of old Converse! Its walls were rough and bumpy but its floor was shiny stone. Not shiny from polish or because it was new, but rather because it was ancient. Countless feet must have felt its cool touch as they'd left their stories. And now it was Bryony's turn to add hers.

She smiled as she spotted the old rocking chair nestled in a deep alcove. It fitted so well, just like it belonged. Like it had been there for ever ...

Suddenly, her thoughts returned to home. To the place where the chair had rocked before. To the busy city – full of noise and cars – where people bustled and lights in shop windows burned all day and night. To their thin white house, with its smooth slate roof and strawberry-red front door. Dad had changed it from black to surprise Mum one day when she'd gone shopping. And it really did as she'd almost walked right past it!

The kitchen in Plum Cottage, although still bare, was very snug and welcoming. When Bryony walked in, Mum was at the Aga in a stripy top and dungarees. Her light brown hair was in a loose wispy bun and round her wrist jangled several silver bangles. She looked arty and very pretty, Bryony thought.

'Hmm ...' said Mum, peering into the Aga. 'Just figuring out how to light the thing!'

'It looks *ancient*,' frowned Josh.

'The colour's nice, though!' smiled Bryony. It was a deep, mysterious navy.

'Yes!' Mum nodded. 'I was just thinking that too.'

It would be easier here, Bryony told herself, than back in the city without Dad. In fact, this funny old place was already starting to weave its magic. She saw her dad's grin in the knots on the doors, in the curls of peeling wallpaper, in the plum trees waving, calling her to play. New adventures were out there waiting too, in the wood and the caves by the sea! Secrets were waiting for her to discover. New friends to make. She was ready ...

'If only it would stop raining!' Bryony said to her mum. 'I want to go and explore! But what if this place hasn't got any *girls*? Just tons of toast-thieving *boys* like my brother?!'

With that, she staged a spectacular faint onto the kitchen table. Great practice, thought Bryony, for when she was an actress!

'Right,' said Mum, bringing over some toast. 'Thank goodness for the toaster! No butter, though – sorry. I'll go shopping later. But we do have jam and—' Suddenly Mum stopped as there was a knock on the door and the twins jumped up and raced each other over shouting ...

'Grandpa!'

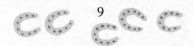

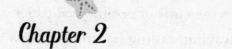

Chapter 2

The next few hours passed happily. It was great to see Grandpa again. He lived down a lane near the sea, just a ten-minute walk through the beech wood at the end of the twins' garden.

For the rest of the morning Grandpa helped them unpack. Though Josh mostly just *pretended* to be unpacking whilst sneakily polishing off the chocolate biscuits that Grandpa had brought for their tea break.

'Now,' said Grandpa just before lunch, 'who's up for a little walk? We could even take a picnic to the caves?'

'But it's pouring!' cried Mum.

'Ah,' smiled Grandpa. 'We country folk don't fuss about the weather!'

'Right, then,' Josh nodded, 'I'm definitely in!' He could remember the caves from when they used to visit Grandpa before. But they'd never gone for a *picnic* in them.

'What about you, Bryony?' Mum asked.

'Are you coming too?' said Bryony. Since Dad had died Bryony had tried to be around more for Mum in case she was lonely.

Mum winked. 'Don't you worry about me, I'll be fine staying here to do a bit more unpacking.'

She turned to Grandpa. 'And I've got just the thing for that picnic!'

Delving around in yet another box, Mum fished out an unopened packet of jam tarts, a big bag of raisins and some crisps.

'I know what moving's like,' she smiled. 'Too busy unpacking to go to the shops, so *this* time I came prepared. Except, of course, for the butter and milk!'

Mum's house move before this one had been to the city, when the twins had been almost five. She hadn't thought to take any provisions then, not even toilet paper! But it hadn't mattered that much as there'd been lots of shops open all

hours. Not here, though. As they'd driven in last night the place had been quiet and almost in complete darkness.

Mum rifled through another of the boxes. 'But where did I put the picnic basket? Huh!' she tutted. 'Just when I was doing so well!'

Quickly Bryony came to the rescue. Hurrying upstairs, she came back down clutching her old riding school rucksack.

'Don't worry,' she said, stuffing the picnic into that. 'All sorted!'

The three of them left, splashing off through the rain into the beech wood at the bottom of the garden. Grandpa explained that, as well as a shortcut to his old fisherman's cottage, the beech wood was also a shortcut to the sea.

How funny, thought Bryony, getting to places *through a wood*. The city where they'd lived before had had great big parks with formal gardens and fountains, but no woods. And back there everyone stuck firmly to the pavements (when they weren't in their high-rise office blocks)!

In this wood, though, the *trees* were the tallest things around, like a vast green tent sheltering

them from the rain. And the breeze sent a pixie-like whisper through the leaves, light and playful and mischievous!

'Hey, Gramps,' cried Josh suddenly. 'Witches' butter – over there!' He pointed and hurried Grandpa over to investigate. Josh had been very into fungi in the city, not that the parks there had had much. The odd toadstool, Bryony recalled, and that was about it, really.

Josh and Grandpa were likely to be *ages* examining this feast of fungi. A wicked yellow colour, it was smothering the fallen tree stump just beyond.

While they did that, Bryony wandered on collecting bits from the woodland floor: feathers, pretty leaves, interesting bits of bark and the odd unripe beech nut. She squirrelled these away into the pocket of her rucksack. Later on she'd make them into some kind of dangly toy thing for Blueberry!

As she walked, Bryony became aware of the wind. It was steadily growing louder and more blustery all the time. Maybe, she thought, being close to the sea meant that the weather here changed more rapidly?

13

She looked up. The treetops were now blowing about, letting raindrops through in patchy splatters. And the ferns on the woodland floor were suddenly swishing and swaying about like an angry sea. Even so, it was really beautiful. Becky and Fran would be so jealous when they visited!

But then, above the rain and the rustle of the leaves, Bryony heard another sound. She stopped. Dead still. Scarcely breathing.

Was that a *pony* whinnying?

Or was it just the wind?

She listened harder. All was quiet. A wood pigeon flapped away. Nothing. It was nothing after all.

But then she heard it again. And this time the sound was unmistakable. It was! It really *was* the sound of a pony.

As if in a trance, she followed it, wading through the wet ferns. A little further, and further still, she went, the whinnying getting louder all the time.

Finally she peeped through a gap in the trees into a small clearing beyond. And there he was! Bryony's heart skipped a beat; the most adorable little bay pony she'd ever seen!

But the pony looked spooked. He was rearing up, his ears flat back and his long black tail thrashing about.

Bryony saw a girl run after him into the clearing. She was breathless and looked very scared. She halted well back and, trembling, she slipped behind a tree to watch him. Bryony guessed that her pony must have thrown her, then bolted. And now the girl was too shaken to get any closer and catch him.

'Hello!' called Bryony, but the girl didn't hear. Bryony waited until the pony stopped rearing then glanced back at his owner again. The girl still looked terrified. Bryony knew that feeling. She had been thrown before too. But someone needed to calm the pony down . . .

Slowly Bryony edged forward through the ferns, hoping to catch the pony's eye. It would be far less scary for him if he saw her coming.

He suddenly spotted her and clattered back, though he didn't rear up like before. Bryony stood still again. She heard the wind moan. She knew lots of ponies were scared by the wind, and this storm had come on so quickly it wasn't any wonder he was spooked. His snorts were loud and

15

very high-pitched and his ears were twitching and flying about in panic.

'It's all right . . .' Bryony called to him, her voice soft and calm. He didn't hear. She called again, and this time both his ears shot to face the direction of her voice.

'Yes, that's the way,' Bryony said. The pony was listening and watching her now.

'I'm just going to come across and help, okay?'

Nice and steadily, she started moving towards him again. She saw out of the corner of her eye that his owner was still paralysed with fear. If anyone was to calm the pony now it must be Bryony . . .

As soon as she was close enough, Bryony looked for a lead rein, but he didn't appear to be wearing one. So slowly reaching out, she took his reins instead, making sure to keep them nice and relaxed so the bit inside his mouth didn't hurt him. The pony snorted nervously but didn't try to tug away. 'Well done,' said Bryony gently. 'Good boy.'

Being so close, Bryony was now struck by his gorgeous big brown eyes. Yet *behind* those eyes – Bryony glimpsed it at once – there was something

16

else. The same something she glimpsed behind her *own* eyes sometimes when she caught her reflection in a mirror or shop window. She hadn't, until now, realised what that something was. It was sadness.

Keeping very still, Bryony spoke to the pony calmly and reassuringly. 'Hello there. That's right, no need to be scared. I'm Bryony, and that sound – it's only the wind, it won't hurt you.'

The pony looked back at Bryony, like he was weighing her up. Keeping hold of his reins in one hand, Bryony reached out the other for the pony to sniff. He stayed still for a moment. Then his head leaned in closer and as he started to sniff Bryony's fingers she could feel his warm breath.

'Good to meet you,' she murmured. 'I'm Bryony.'

The pony gave a deep gentle blow but he still looked unsure. Bryony slowly moved her hand to the side of his neck and started to stroke it, keeping a steady rhythm and talking to him all the time in soft, low whispers.

Eventually she felt his body relax and his breathing become more even. 'I'm a friend,' she whispered, and to her delight the pony edged a little closer. 'There, that's right. What a *brave* boy,' she said.

Bryony noticed a small starry-shaped patch in between the pony's eyes.

'Oh!' she gasped – suddenly remembering that her dad used to call *her* his little star. It was almost as if she and this pony had been destined to meet.

The pony's owner appeared at Bryony's side. Her face was ghostly-white and she was still trembling.

'Are you okay?' asked Bryony, and the girl managed a nod.

'A-and thanks so much,' she replied. 'I don't know what I would have done without you. I'm Emma, by the way.'

'I'm . . .'

'. . . Bryony!' The girl finished Bryony's sentence. 'I just heard you tell the pony. By the way, I think you're amazing with him.'

'Oh, not really.' Bryony blushed. 'I'm just a bit pony-mad, that's all, and read pony books all the time. They give me tips on things to try out, you know?'

Just then, above the deep wet rustle of the trees, Bryony heard the sound of footsteps.

'Bry!' called her brother from one side of the wood. And . . .

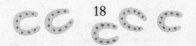

18

'Emma!' came a girl's voice from the other.

Bryony then saw a girl with white-blonde hair heading through the tangle of trees. She assumed this girl was Emma's friend and that they'd lost each other when Emma's pony had bolted.

Emma saw her friend too and turned back to Bryony . . .

'Sorry, I've got to go!' she said quickly.

'But—' began Bryony.

'Bye!' Emma called, already leading her pony away. 'And thanks again for stepping in just now. See you!'

Bryony did hope she'd see Emma again too as she'd seemed really nice.

'Wait – Emma! Where do you live?' called Bryony but the wind whipped her words away. Then Josh and Grandpa appeared in the clearing.

'Hey, come see the fungi!' grinned Josh.

'I just need to do something first,' replied Bryony, looking round for Emma again. But Emma, her friend and the beautiful bay pony had vanished.

*

Even the darkest and spookiest of caves didn't stop Bryony thinking about what had happened in the beech wood. She really wanted to find Emma again. She was sure they'd get on well, especially as they had *ponies* in common.

As for her pony – he was gorgeous! Never before had Bryony felt such a strong connection with a pony.

She thought of his special little star, and the way he'd trusted and responded to her. And those eyes, with the hint of *sadness* behind them. But why would he be sad with such a nice owner as Emma?

After their picnic in the caves, the twins and Grandpa poked around in the rock pools and explored under the pier.

Bryony could remember the beach a bit from when they used to visit Grandpa before. But back then they'd been quite little, and after that Dad had got ill so Grandpa had come to visit *them* instead. This meant that Bryony's memories of Brook Dale were quite hazy and distant now. All the more exciting to rediscover it!

As they left the beach the sun was out, and with it came more people. They were climbing some

old stone steps back up to the prom when they bumped into a boy walking his bulldog. The boy, Bryony thought, looked about their age and was wearing a hoodie and the latest flashy trainers. His dog looked grumpy, as did the boy at having to stop to let them pass.

'Cool dog!' smiled Josh.

'Hmm,' grunted the boy. 'You're not from round 'ere, are you?'

The boy's bulldog was straining on its lead and space was very tight so Grandpa and Bryony continued up the steps as Josh answered him.

As Bryony waited with Grandpa on the prom, she looked around at the sights. The place might be small but it was very pretty. In front of them was the lovely sandy beach, and behind them was 'town' and rolling green hills dotted with whitewashed cottages that looked like sheep!

Bryony also saw the harbour with its neat rows of fishing boats. And jutting into the sea in the distance was the headland, on which, as well as an old disused lighthouse, there looked to be a *new* building too. Bryony narrowed her eyes, just able to make out some children on *ponies* going into it.

'Gramps!' She pointed. 'Is that a riding stable?'

'Ah, yes,' answered Grandpa as Josh joined them. 'A *brand new* riding stable too. It's called Seaview Stables and it's—'

'Not like you've got your own *pony*, though, is it?' Josh chipped in, without thinking.

Bryony felt her face fall and Josh must have seen it too because suddenly he went quiet and looked really awkward.

'I didn't mean . . .' Josh shuffled. 'You could still *go* there though, right?'

'It's okay,' replied Bryony, though quickly realising it didn't *feel* okay at all.

Josh was right. She *didn't* have her own pony. Or a bedroom that felt like hers. And what if she didn't make any *friends* here either?

Bryony quickly blinked back the tears she could feel pooling in her eyes. If she let herself cry, she might never stop. And that felt very scary . . .

As they walked back through the beech wood, she listened for a pony in case Emma was still about. But this time it really was just the wind that she heard.

They arrived at Plum Cottage around teatime.

Mum was out in the front garden eating a plum from one of their trees.

'Hello! How was the walk?' she asked. She was sitting on an old wooden bench, bare-footed, her canvas shoes lying on the grass. Threaded into her bun was a small yellow rose from the overgrown bush beside her.

'Great caves,' grinned Josh. 'And there's *fungi* in the woods! As soon as I find the tent I'm camping out there.'

'How about you, love?' Mum looked at Bryony.

'I . . . I met a girl with a pony,' answered Bryony. Josh looked puzzled.

'When?' Grandpa asked.

'When you and Josh were looking at the witches' butter. But then she had to go before I could give her our address,' replied Bryony.

Grandpa was very good at reading feelings. He caught Bryony's eye and winked.

'I'm *sure* you'll meet her again, love,' he said. 'That's the thing with little seaside towns – no one's ever that far away.'

'Yes, I guess so . . .' Bryony nodded. She did hope Grandpa was right.

23

'Right, then!' said Josh. 'What's for supper, Mum?'

'Josh, it's *hours* till supper time!' Mum laughed.

'Well, I can definitely recommend the fish and chip shop,' grinned Grandpa. ''Tis run by Saul Salmon, the fisherman!'

'*And ...*' Grandpa looked at the cat on the window ledge, supremely ignoring the world, '... it *even* does scraps for rather grumpy moggies!'

Chapter 3

The next day was beautifully sunny. Just the weather to *not* unpack! Instead, Bryony offered to go to the shops and post a parcel that her mum needed sending. It was a birthday present for Mum's sister, Bryony's aunt. Her mother had just found it buried deep in a packing box, already wrapped in brown paper, and Bryony was glad of the excuse to go off and post it.

'Wait, do you even know the way?' Mum called as Bryony headed out of the door.

'I'll work it out!' Bryony called back. 'Can't be hard!'

She knew, from yesterday, she could go through the wood which would bring her out at the beach. Then she could backtrack uphill to the main street.

But Emma, she thought, might well live in one of the cottages on the longer way to town, so that's the way she finally decided to go.

The front garden of Plum Cottage tumbled onto a narrow country lane. On the far side of this was a babbling brook that gambolled along beside it, like a puppy following its every twist and turn!

As Bryony walked on, the sound of bees filled the air and the hedgerows were crammed with lacy cow parsley bending lazily into her path. The air wore the perfume of summer too, made stronger after yesterday's rain. Deep green grass, frilly flowers and moist brown earth filled Bryony's lungs with the deep mysterious potions of the countryside. A busy ladybird scuttling along a wall, a frog springing across the lane and a paper-thin butterfly drifting by on the breeze made her feel like she was walking through the most beautiful dream!

Presently the lane widened out and a cluster of small cottages came into view. Their gardens were jam-packed with sweet-smelling flowers that spread out like a pretty patchwork quilt. Stocks, and delphiniums, and tall swaying hollyhocks. Bryony knew all the names from last term's school

project. Plus, before her dad had died her mum had been a florist. She'd had a break from it for a little while but Bryony hoped Mum would go back to it once they'd settled into Brook Dale.

Passing the cottages (with sadly no sign of Emma), Bryony followed the lane as it swept her around a dusty bend. After this, the lane became more of a road, with narrow pavements on either side. Walking on up a twisty hill, Bryony soon found herself in what she could only guess was Brook Dale's main street.

'Wow!' said Bryony. She'd arrived in town. *If* you could call it that. Ancient and magical – this place was so different to the city's wide, shop-lined streets. It looked like no other place she'd ever seen before. Like it belonged on a Christmas card!

The pavements were cobbled and the houses here had lost their quaint cottagey look, being much taller, thinner, and rather wonky!

They were not all whitewashed either, like the cottages up on the hills were. These houses had been painted soft ice cream colours: strawberry-pink, vanilla-yellow and a pale mint-green.

A few of them had shops on their ground floor

and the owners lived above. Others were smaller and Bryony guessed that these ones must just be houses. Finally, burrowing between each of them was a rabbit warren of tangled lanes, leading to smaller, much artier shops behind.

The song of seagulls now filled the air and the smell of the beautiful cottage flowers had been replaced by a salty sea-tang.

Halfway down the street stood the fishmonger's (which was also the fish and chip shop at night!). And beside it was an ancient coaching inn called The Bear and Porridge Pot.

Next to that, Bryony was pleased to find the very shop she was after. She read the tin sign propped up against its wall: *The Old Post Office and Grocery Store.*

It was a white building, rather like you'd see in Tudor times, with black beams that criss-crossed, and one big one across the top of the door.

Bryony stepped onto the old smooth step. Meeting new people was always a bit daunting so she took a few deep, calming breaths like she'd been taught in drama club. Then, gingerly, she opened the small creaky door.

Ting ting! Its top hit a little bell inside, which tinkled a cheery welcome. Bryony edged into the cool, polish-scented air and waited.

The place was empty. And no one seemed to be serving. But Bryony *loved* the look of it. It felt like she'd just stepped back in time, or was an actress in a film – set hundreds of years ago. It had wooden floorboards and the window was made up of lots of small thick panes of glass, which made the street outside look all wobbly and melted.

It had wooden shelves too, and tubs of ice cream in square blocks of colour, like a paintbox! As Bryony waited for the shopkeeper to appear, she decided to have a quick snoop round. The shop seemed to sell anything and everything. There was fruit and veg, and a whole shelf of home-made jams of various flavours. Their lids were covered with gingham hats tied with neat ribbons. There were balls of wool, *hundreds* of coloured threads, as well as crabbing nets and socks. On the wall behind the old-fashioned till were three very long shelves. Lining each shelf was a row of glass jars full of traditional sweets – liquorice and sherbet lemons and mints with brown stripes.

To the side of these jars was a latched pine door on which hung an old cork noticeboard. Pinned to this board were a number of dog-eared cards.

Bryony read the notices on each of the cards. Most of them were advertising things for sale. A bike, a wooden castle (with a dragon and some knights), an assortment of nearly new baby clothes. By the crumpled, yellowed look of the cards and their faded writing, most of these notices looked like they'd been there a while.

Bryony's eyes were then drawn to a card that looked much newer and smarter.

WANTED

My ten-year-old daughter has a new pony and needs a friend to help her with him.
Anyone interested please call Arabella Brook.

07798 771 225

'Wow! What if it's *the* pony?' Bryony blurted out. 'The one I met yesterday in the beech wood!' And the girl she'd met – what if *she* was Emma Brook?

Then Bryony recalled the girl w...

blonde hair who had been with Emma too. ...

already *had* a friend to help her with the pony. ...

Bryony's heart sank. That blonde girl must have

got to this 'WANTED' card first. 'But who says

you can't have *two* friends?' said Bryony. 'Or three,

or four, or quite as many friends as you like!'

Just then, the latch on the pine door lifted and

a wrinkled old lady shuffled through. She was

wearing a flowery apron and tartan slippers with

pompoms on.

"Ooo you gabbing to?' the old lady snapped,

peering around the empty shop.

'Um, no one,' Bryony squeaked back, going pink.

The old lady was as bony as a billy goat, with

as hairy a chin as well! She had wispy, snow-white

hair pulled back into a neat bun, and big owl-like

eyes, except hers were violet blue.

'Ah, but you're the *new* girl!' she cackled. "Bout

time an' all! I knew you was coming to live 'ere –

for months and months, you know!'

Bryony said nothing. But the old lady couldn't

have! Even *Mum* hadn't known that ...

'I'm Miss Pigeon!' the old lady went on,

unscrewing a glass jar behind her and taking out two sticks of liquorice. One she gave to Bryony who thanked her, puzzled, and the other she popped behind her very wrinkly left ear.

'And Pigeon *is* me real name before you goes asking!' the old lady said with a nod. Despite trying to look stern, her violet-blue eyes were twinkling.

'I'm Bryony – um, Mr Wallace's granddaughter,' Bryony replied uncertainly.

''Course you are!' Miss Pigeon grinned. 'I'm a fortune-teller. Well, part time, you knows, when I'm not serving in 'ere. And like I said, I *knew* you was coming – and 'ere yer are!'

Bryony blinked. A fortune-teller? Huh! More likely Grandpa *told* her they were coming, she thought, but she didn't dare *say* it!

Instead, Bryony held her parcel out.

'I'd, um ... like to post this parcel to my auntie,' she said.

''Course you would!' Miss Pigeon nodded back. 'I knew that too!'

She took the parcel and thumped it down on an ancient set of weighing scales. Now sucking on the liquorice from behind her left ear, Miss Pigeon

popped a stamp on the parcel (upside down!). Then Bryony paid her, but instead of leaving, she stood there awkwardly hovering ...

'Err, Miss Pigeon ...' Bryony said. 'Can I borrow a pencil and some paper, please?'

"Course you can, dearie!' Miss Pigeon answered. 'I *knew* you was going to ask me that so – 'ere!'

She whipped a scrap of paper from her apron pocket and a small brown pencil to go with it.

'Thanks!' said Bryony as the old lady passed them over.

'Aye.'

Bryony got the distinct feeling that if Miss Pigeon liked you, you were fine. But, if she didn't, watch out!

Bryony copied down the details from the 'WANTED' card and handed the pencil back. 'Thanks.'

'Ah, so you likes *ponies*, do you?' asked Miss Pigeon, nodding to the card on the door.

'Yes!' Bryony nodded back. 'Very much!'

'Aye, well, you know what?' Miss Pigeon winked. 'There's a riding stables 'ere, there is. Up on them cliffs. Seaview Stables, it's called.'

'Y-yes ...' Bryony smiled and was about to say, *I know*, when suddenly she stopped. Miss Pigeon was clearly trying to be kind. And even if the *only* one who believed she could read the future was the old lady herself, it wouldn't harm for Bryony to play along and make her feel good.

'Oh, great!' gasped Bryony. 'Thanks for ... telling me. You must have known I was *just* about to ask that!'

'Aye – nice spot,' Miss Pigeon beamed. 'Though right windy in winter. And summer too when a storm comes.'

'I don't mind wind!' Bryony's green eyes were twinkling. If she did become a friend of Emma Brook now that she had her phone number, they could ride the pony along the beach. And Bryony could visit the riding stables with Emma – and the blonde girl too. The more the merrier!

Waving goodbye to Miss Pigeon, Bryony hurried to the door. It suddenly felt like she was walking on air!

'Have a nice day!' Miss Pigeon called after her.

'You too!' called Bryony. 'And thank you!'

Running back along the cobbled street, Bryony's

heart was beating fast. She was going to get *a friend with a pony*. This was perfect!

'Mum!' she cried, dashing into Plum Cottage. She waved her scrap of paper in the air.

'Mum – please can you phone this number? I found it in the shop just now! Remember I told you about that girl? The one I saw in the wood yesterday? Well, it turns out she needs a friend to help look after her new pony! And—'

'Whoa, slow down a bit!' Her mother smiled.

'But it's *Emma*!' cried Bryony, already dialling the number. She jabbed the phone back at her mum.

'Ask if we can meet tomorrow!' nodded Bryony. 'Or today. Or – or – right now!'

Seconds later Mum was talking to someone on the other end of the line. Crossing her fingers tightly, Bryony waited as Mum explained all about Bryony, and how she'd found their number, and how she was longing to make a new friend.

'And tell her I LOVE ponies!' Bryony whispered.

'And she really *adores* ponies,' said her mum.

'Yes,' said Mum. 'Oh, I see. Yes, that would be lovely! Um, thank you, Arabella. Okay then – we'll see you next Wednesday at two. Bye!'

Mum hung up.

'Yay!' cried Bryony. 'We're going round! But I have to wait until *Wednesday*?'

'That's right,' smiled Mum. 'It's only five days away. Arabella's invited us for tea!'

'Did she sound nice?' Bryony asked.

'Yes,' Mum nodded. 'She said that they'd bought their daughter this sweet pony.'

'E-Emma,' said Bryony. 'They'd bought *Emma* the pony?'

'Um …' Mum thought. 'I'm not sure if she mentioned her daughter's name …'

'It must be Emma,' Bryony smiled. 'It just must!'

Bryony spent the next four days unpacking and finding places on the uneven walls to stick up all her pony posters (there were lots!). This she did without a single complaint as she replayed the scene over and over in her head of when she and Emma would meet again, and of course when she saw the gorgeous little pony again too.

It suddenly dawned on her that she didn't even know the pony's name. Anyway, she'd soon find out. And Mum, she thought, might make a new friend too – Arabella!

On the evening before the tea party, Bryony took herself out to the garden. The air was warm and balmy and she loved being in a place so wonderfully wild and untouched.

Bryony waded through the tall, dry grass which tickled her bare legs. Deep within it she imagined a myriad of tiny creatures hiding out in their cool earthy jungle – snails and slugs and busy little ants getting on with their evening unwatched by human eyes.

She made her way to an ancient swing hanging from one of the plum trees near the shed. She had spied this swing the other day but hadn't had the time to try it out then. Now, with the loveliest peach and lilac sunset painting the warm summer's sky, it was definitely the evening to give it a go.

'Right!' smiled Bryony and, brushing off the cobwebs, she climbed onto the old wooden seat.

At first she took things slowly, making sure the swing would hold her weight. Then when she was happy the old ropes wouldn't snap, she decided to see how high she could make it go.

As the swing creaked rhythmically back and fore, Bryony began to think. She thought about

Becky and Fran, wondering what they were up to this summer. No doubt they were down at her old riding school every single day. Perhaps preparing for another gymkhana? Or pony camp.

Bryony used to love the holidays, hanging about Park Lodge Stables. The busy-ness, the chatter, and, of course, the ponies! But there were other, exciting things *here* now, she told herself.

Her thoughts turned to Emma Brook once more. Tomorrow she'd get to see her again. Bryony could hardly wait! And if Emma *did* ride at Seaview Stables, they might even be planning a brilliant Brook Dale gymkhana!

Bryony leaped off the swing in mid-air and raced up into the cottage. In the kitchen she threw on an apron, then rummaged through the cupboards for some baking tins. Emma, she thought, might really like it if she took some cakes along tomorrow. She used to bake a lot with Becky and Fran. And *everyone* – she figured – liked cakes!

In no time at all, the old pine table was laden down with ingredients.

'What you doing?' asked her brother, sloping in from outside.

'Making blueberry muffins for tomorrow!'

'Oh, yeah,' Josh tutted. 'That tea party. Got better things to do, I have.'

'Like what?' asked Bryony.

'Ah,' smiled Josh. 'Well, I'm meeting Dartt – my new mate,' he added. 'And, err . . . a couple of the others.'

'Hang on,' said Bryony, opening the flour. 'Who's Dartt and *a couple of the others*?'

Her brother clapped the flour bag (she should have seen *that* coming) and fell about laughing as Bryony was suddenly engulfed in a big floury snowstorm.

'Dartt!' Josh repeated. 'You remember – last week – the boy at the beach with the bulldog?'

Bryony snatched up the box of eggs her brother was now eyeing menacingly. She did remember the boy with the dog – now, apparently, her brother's 'mate'.

''Course his real name's not Dartt,' Josh continued, looking around for something else to explode. 'Dan Artt, he's called. But, you know – he's *Dartt* to me and the gang.'

At that moment, Mum appeared. 'Ah, Josh, I've

been looking for you,' she said. 'There's a mountain of clothes all over your floor. Time to find homes for them, I think.'

'But, Mum, can't I help Bryony instead? I'm *egg*cellent at cracking eggs!'

Mum shook her head and, sensing he was beaten, Josh trooped off to the stairs.

'Wardrobes,' he grumbled. 'Complete waste of time, if you ask me!'

As Bryony made the muffins it struck her that Josh seemed somehow different tonight. A bit edgy – and boasty about his new gang. Well, by this time tomorrow, *she'd* have a new friend too!

When the muffin mixture was (fairly) smooth, she spooned it into cases in the baking tin. Then Mum prised the old Aga door open and Bryony carefully popped the tin inside.

While she waited for the muffins to bake Bryony's thoughts turned to Dad once more. She often used to take him her blueberry muffins as he worked.

Bryony's father had been an artist and she'd inherited his passion for creating. But sculpture was probably the thing that they'd both loved most.

Bryony remembered how, when she was little, she'd sit beside him making animals from clay. She remembered how Dad always *loved* them. How he'd line them all up on his easel. Then he'd throw down his brushes and they'd play with them. For hours and hours they'd play! They'd bring them to life. They'd give them voices. Give them happy endings. And this had made Bryony feel special; like she could do anything. Like the little clay ponies, and rabbits, and cats were as priceless as diamonds and rubies. To Dad they were and that was all that mattered ...

When the muffins were baked, Bryony packed them in a biscuit tin all ready to take tomorrow. Then she hurried upstairs to pick out the perfect outfit.

Maybe jeans would be better than a skirt, she thought, in case Emma let her ride the pony.

'Ah! The *pony* ...' Bryony beamed. 'Oh, please, please let him remember me!'

Chapter 4

On Wednesday afternoon, at one o'clock, Bryony was ready to leave.

'It's too early,' grinned Mum.

'I know!' giggled Bryony. 'But I just don't want to be late!'

Clutching her tin of blueberry muffins, she paced around the cottage checking every clock and counting down the minutes. Blueberry Muffin, the cat, eyed the tin hopefully. He *adored* blueberry muffins. In fact, that's how he'd got his name – tracking down (and then wolfing down!) a whole plateful of blueberry muffins in the kitchen the very first night they'd brought him home as a kitten . . .

What felt like *hours* later, it was finally time to

set off. But they'd only just reached the garden gate when it dawned on Bryony that she hadn't a clue where they were heading.

'Mum, where does Emma actually live?' she asked.

'Well, Arabella said on the phone,' replied Mum, 'that their house is called Brook Dale Manor. It's on the outskirts somewhere, down a leafy lane. Anyway, she gave me directions.'

Mum opened the gate and went through.

'But, Mum!' gasped Bryony, quickly following. 'Brook Dale Manor sounds *huge*.' She glanced down at her jeans, now looking really tatty.

'Don't worry,' Mum laughed, nudging her arm. 'You look fine!'

A frustrating walk later (they got *very* lost – twice!), Bryony and her mum stood gaping up at the huge iron gates that marked the entrance to Brook Dale Manor. Bryony suddenly found she had butterflies turning *somersaults* in her tummy.

'Look at the garden!' she gasped, peeping in. 'The flowers! There must be millions!' She'd never seen anything quite like it before.

And the lawn looked as vast as an ocean, its surface

velvety soft. No weeds, no tufts, it shimmered in the sun. A little *too* perfect, perhaps ...

An enormous curved wall framed the gates, into which was set an intercom. 'Right, here goes. Are you ready?' asked Mum.

'Ready if you are,' breathed Bryony.

Bryony pressed the button then leaped back, as if she'd just been bitten. They heard a click, then a man's voice spoke in calm, measured phrases.

'Good afternoon. Welcome to Brook Dale Manor. Please come inside.'

'How does he—' Bryony began. But then she saw a little camera mounted on top of the gates and fixed, very firmly, on their faces. With a whirr and a clunk, the iron gates swept open and Bryony and her mum hurried through.

The white gravelled driveway led up to the house in an elegant sweeping curve, like the long trailing veil of a bride.

'*Look*, they've even got peacocks!' Bryony whispered, as three strutted past in a line. A line so straight it was hard to believe they were real.

The manor house was palatial. Its symmetry made it look like a doll's house, but one that had grown to *gigantic* proportions – like something out of the pages of *Alice in Wonderland*. Bryony gazed around taking everything in, and half expecting to spot a tall, well-dressed, white rabbit!

They climbed a flight of wide stone steps leading up to the huge front door. The door opened and to their great relief, a friendly-looking face beamed out. Bryony felt her body relax. It was going to be all right. Arabella Brook looked really lovely!

'Hello there!' she said.

'Hello,' replied Mum. 'I'm Elizabeth May, and this is Bryony, my daughter.'

'Do come in!' Arabella smiled. 'I'm Bella!'

She ushered them into a high-ceilinged hallway where everything sparkled and shone. The tiles on the floor were tumbled marble and the wallpaper, wild silk. Bryony had never seen anything so beautiful.

Then, suddenly, down the large sweeping staircase, came Bella's daughter. Bryony gasped, for she knew her at once. Not Emma! It was the *other* girl. The girl with white-blonde hair. The one who'd been calling for Emma that day in the beech wood.

For a moment, Bryony felt disappointed. She'd been certain Bella's daughter would be Emma.

45

But, as the girl drew closer, Bryony thought that at least she should give this other girl a chance.

Bryony walked towards her, smiling. 'Hi!' she said. 'I'm Bryony.'

'Ah,' replied the girl. 'I'm Georgina Brook.'

Georgina Brook was very pretty. Her skin was as pale as porcelain and her nose turned up and small. She looked just like a priceless china doll.

Bryony then noticed Georgina's eyes, a pale shade of aquamarine, which, according to Bryony's gemstone book, was the colour of friendship and trust. That had to be a really good sign!

Bella showed them into the drawing room. 'Please,' she smiled, 'do come in and sit down!'

The dark panelled walls of this room were adorned with ornate oil paintings, and a grand piano sat on the polished wooden floor.

The French doors had all been opened wide and a perfumed breeze fluttered in. As well as filling the air with the smell of lavender, it also set the jewels on the huge chandelier tinkling. Bryony watched as they swayed and twirled. They looked just like sparkly ballerinas!

Her gaze finally dropped to her own scruffy

Converse, which this morning had looked okay. Not any more, on these floorboards as shiny as ice!

'Bryony has such lovely hair,' said Bella, looking across the sunny room at its warm rich tones. 'Such beautiful *curls*, and a really pretty colour too!'

'Just like her dad's, her hair,' beamed Mum. 'He was an artist – my husband. He did *amazing* sculptures too! Bryony wants to be an actress, though, don't you, darling?'

Bryony blinked. 'Um, yes!' she said. She couldn't quite take it in. Mum had hardly been able to talk about Dad since he'd died almost six months ago. Not *even*, thought Bryony, to her or Josh.

Each time Mum had tried, it would always *start* okay, but then she'd suddenly turn away, or pretend she'd left something in another room so she had an excuse to nip off. That way, Bryony knew, Mum hoped they wouldn't notice the tears suddenly welling in her eyes. Here today, though – for whatever reason – her mention of Dad had tumbled out so naturally. This was something Bryony had been wanting for so long . . .

'I-I've made some muffins!' Bryony blurted out, offering the tin to Georgina.

'Blueberry,' she went on. 'I really, um ... hope you like them!'

Bryony wasn't sure what happened next. Georgina must have slipped. And as she tried to steady herself, her arm caught Bryony's tin. It soared high up into the air and landed with an ear-splitting clatter, the contents of the tin flying out everywhere.

'Oh! So sorry!' Bryony blushed, scooping up the now broken bits of cake. She felt so silly. Like somehow it had been all *her* fault.

'No harm done, dear,' said Bella quickly, taking the tin now littered with crumbs and bits of broken muffin. 'We'll have them later with our tea. I'm sure they'll still taste lovely! Now, Georgie darling, why not take Bryony to see your new pony, mmm?'

'She may not want to,' Georgina replied.

'Oh, I do!' cried Bryony. 'I *love* ponies, that's why we answered the ad.'

She found herself thinking of Emma's pony again, that gorgeous dark bay that had trusted her. She still had a longing to see him again. There was so much about him that captivated her. But she was curious to see Georgina's new pony too ...

Georgina nodded and Bryony followed her out through the smart French doors. Then, keeping to the paths, they strolled around the lawn as bright little butterflies sunned themselves on the lavender.

'I used to ride a lot,' chattered Bryony. 'Though I've never owned my own pony. It was me that helped Emma the other day. That day her pony bolted in the beech wood.'

'*Her* pony?' Georgina stopped and raised a puzzled white-blonde eyebrow. 'Why, Emma hasn't *got* a pony. You're confused.'

'No, remember?' said Bryony. 'He was scared in all that wind. You were looking for them – calling for Emma. I saw—'

'That pony you saw is *mine*,' Georgina cut in, her voice suddenly ice-cold. She flashed her pale blue eyes at Bryony, clearly rather offended.

'Just so you know,' Georgina continued. '*That* day, Emma Lawrence went to retrieve *my* pony right after he threw—' Georgina stopped. 'Right after he decided to run off from me. There is only *one* pony and I can assure you – he's *mine*.'

Biting her lip, Bryony continued to follow Georgina around the immaculate lawn. A tall

wall surrounded the back garden, in the middle of which was a pretty wrought iron gate. Georgina opened it and they went through and down a twisty tree-lined path. This led to an orchard with trees in neat rows, their branches heavy with apples.

Bryony was waiting for Georgina to speak but Georgina said nothing as she marched through the orchard, presumably, thought Bryony, towards the paddock and stables.

After a while, though, the silence grew so awkward that Bryony decided to try again.

'Well, anyway, your pony – he's amazing!' she said, really meaning it.

'Actually,' Georgina replied with a scowl, 'he's useless.'

Sensing she'd said the wrong thing again, Bryony's heart was sinking fast. If *only* she hadn't mentioned that day in the beech wood!

'I'll help you with him – i-if you like?' Bryony quickly offered, her voice now quiet and uncertain. 'He's probably just not used to you yet . . . as he's new. And unfamiliar surroundings – they probably don't help either. I'm sure, well . . . he'll settle really soon.'

Bryony glanced at Georgina, whose pale cheeks

now flushed magenta. Yet again Bryony sensed she'd made things worse.

'Oh, I *see*,' Georgina was now smirking. 'Don't think I'm up to it, do you? Just because *you* calmed him down that day, you think you're *better* than me?'

'No!' gasped Bryony, horrified. 'It's just . . . I . . . no – I didn't mean—'

'That pony's ridiculous!' Georgina snapped. 'Despite what *you* or *Emma* think. See, *I* would have chosen a far better pony but my parents "surprised" me with *him*. They always think they know what I need. But they don't.'

Georgina stopped at the end of the orchard, but she hadn't quite finished her speech. She turned to look at Bryony beside the gate.

'The thing is, I'm perfectly capable,' said Georgina in a sweetly dangerous voice, 'not only of choosing my own *pony*, but of choosing my own *friends* too!'

'Oh . . .' Bryony sighed. She'd got the message. This was never going to work. Georgina wasn't going to be her friend, whatever she said, or did. She might as well stop now and head back home.

But then suddenly she heard it . . . the *tap, tap, tap*

of a little hoof. It was *him*. The pony was calling – calling *her*. And Bryony knew – she couldn't leave. Not now.

Racing through the gate, Bryony followed the pony's call. She ran past the paddock. It was empty, so she continued to the stables beyond.

When she got there, Bryony looked around. There were three stable doors, two of which were shut. The third, however, had its top door open and Bryony could see the pony inside. His back was to her, his head bent low and his glossy black tail hanging down limp. Bryony gasped. He looked so sad and lonely!

'*Hello*,' she said softly, feeling a flutter in her tummy just at seeing him again. The pony must have heard, for he shuffled slightly and raised his head a little. Bryony waited patiently for him to turn around.

The air smelled familiar, like Bryony's old riding school: the sweet smell of hay and leather. Yet every pony had their own *special* smell too, and this little one was no different. Bryony breathed it in. Now, what did it remind her of . . .?

There was definitely a hint of oats, but this pony smelled of *cinnamon* as well. The smell took Bryony back to a cake shop in the city called Clara's. She used to go there every Saturday as a treat right after her riding lesson. And the cakes and fancy pastries smelled just delicious!

The pony now turned and their eyes met, hers green like the sea and his an earthy brown. In the beech wood last week their meeting had been rushed. But now Bryony could really appreciate how beautiful he was . . .

His deep brown coat was the colour of chocolate. And his lower legs matched his mane and tail, which were black. His mane stuck up in cute tufts or tumbled playfully over his eyes. And just above the white star in the middle of his face bounced a single little black kiss curl.

Now that she was here and had met Georgina, Bryony had no doubt what was making this pony sad. He was simply desperate to be loved . . .

He clattered over to the door and leaned his head towards Bryony. As he did, he gave a soft, curious blow and his eyes examined her face.

'You *do* know me . . .' Bryony whispered. 'Remember?'

For a moment the pony stood there thoughtfully.

Then his ears, still lying flat back against his head, slowly began to straighten and his eyes opened and twinkled. 'Ah!' beamed Bryony. He did! He *did* remember her!

'See?' scowled Georgina, appearing in the yard. 'Useless little beast!'

'He *isn't*,' hissed Bryony, trying to stay calm as a sudden surge of hate towards Georgina began to bubble deep in her tummy. This feeling was unfamiliar and very unsettling. Bryony had never before hated anyone.

But Georgina was wrong. This pony *wasn't* useless. He was clever – and curious, and *loving*!

From the moment they'd met in the beech wood, he'd listened. Just like he was listening now. Letting out a soft excited blow, the pony nuzzled Bryony's arm.

'Oh!' Bryony's heart melted. 'Hello to you too . . .' she whispered back.

Bryony stroked the little white star between his eyes. How could Georgina think badly of him? If only she'd just give him a chance!

The pony gave a light-hearted nicker as if to say: 'Clever *you* for finding me again.'

'Ha! And clever you!' Bryony smiled. 'For *remembering* me!'

'What are you *doing*?' Georgina frowned. 'He can't understand what you're saying!'

Bryony felt herself bristle but didn't reply. It was stiflingly hot in the stable yard and there was a light sheen of sweat on the pony's coat.

'Why is he shut away,' asked Bryony, 'on such a beautiful day? Why isn't he outside nibbling the grass in the paddock?'

'That's up to me,' Georgina replied coolly. 'I don't need *your* advice.'

'I know, but, Georgina – please,' begged Bryony, 'let him come out for a while. I'm not trying to take over, I promise, but, *please*, Georgina?'

Georgina smiled. 'Hmmm ... maybe,' she sniffed, weighing Bryony up like a cat taunts a mouse. 'Though to be honest there's not much point. All he does is tap, tap, tap all day.'

'That's because he's bored!' Bryony gasped. 'And he knows that you don't ... *like* him. He'd do anything you ask if you were just kind.'

Bryony looked at the pony. 'It's all right,' she whispered, stroking him between his ears. She

must have hit a ticklish spot, for suddenly he let out a frilly little snort and his left ear flopped to the side. He had such a loving nature. Why couldn't Georgina *see* it?

'What's his name?' asked Bryony.

'He hasn't got one,' replied Georgina. 'Call him "Nothing" if you like. Nothing's all he's good for, after all!'

Bryony felt like hitting her, but that wouldn't do any good. For *now*, she had to do things Georgina's way . . .

'You said you might let him out?' said Bryony.

'And so I might,' grinned Georgina. 'But he can only come out if you promise me something first.'

'*What?*' cried Bryony. 'Promise you what? *Tell me!*'

'Hmm . . . well,' said Georgina, taking her time. 'The deal's quite simple, really. You must *forget* that ad in the post office. If my mum – or yours, for that matter – asks if you want to come here again, you have to say "no". Make up an excuse. Anything. *You* want to be the actress, after all! Say you hated the stupid pony or—'

'No!' cried Bryony. 'I won't lie! I *won't* say I hated the pony!'

'*Fine,*' said Georgina. 'Then he stays cooped up. Poor thing.'

With that, Georgina turned on her heel and began to stroll away, but the little pony nuzzled Bryony's arm again.

'Georgina!' yelled Bryony. 'All right, I promise! I'll *lie* if that's what it takes. Now, please, Georgina – *please* let me open the door.'

Georgina turned back. She was smirking, her dainty lips as cold as her eyes. 'That's more like it! Go on then – you *may* open the door,' agreed Georgina. 'But don't go getting too attached. Last time you'll ever visit, don't forget!' And raising her eyebrows, Georgina marched off leaving Bryony and the pony alone.

It could have been an hour, or it could have been ten minutes, Bryony lost all track of time. She led the little pony out to the paddock and as soon as he saw the luscious green grass, his fluffy little ears flicked forward. Bryony smiled. At last! He looked so happy!

'And now,' said Bryony, patting his side, 'off you go and explore. Go on – the whole paddock is *yours*. Have fun!'

At first the pony looked uncertain. Like he wasn't sure what to do. So Bryony did a little gallopy run. 'And you!'

The pony seemed thoughtful, then he started to trot. Slowly at first. But as he got more confident he started to pick his hooves up higher – as if doing a funny little dance.

'Trit-trot, trit-trot! Yes! That's the way!' smiled Bryony.

Eventually he began a wide circuit of the paddock, like he needed to stretch his powerful muscles after being cooped up for so long. He kept coming up to Bryony to check she was still there and then trotting off again. It was so great to see him do whatever he pleased!

Finally he came to a stop near Bryony and nuzzled her shoulder with his velvety muzzle.

'A tickle?' giggled Bryony. 'Just behind the ears?' The pony looked hopeful.

'Okay, sure!'

As she tickled him, just like before, his left ear suddenly flopped to the side. Now he'd learned what *tickles* were it was like he never wanted them to stop!

Before she could stop herself, Bryony was imagining that this little pony was *hers*. Imagining they had all summer to run free and explore Brook Dale together. So much more fun than exploring it on her own. The leafy lanes, the woods, the fields, the hills were all out there waiting for them! And she'd never ridden *any* pony along a beach before. How amazing would it be to do it for the first time on *this* pony?

The daydream ended in a flash of white-blonde hair. Georgina Brook was striding back through the orchard.

Bryony rested her head on the pony's side, feeling his heart beating. The afternoon sunshine was dancing on his coat, bringing out rich deep red tones.

'Don't believe her,' Bryony whispered to him. 'Don't listen when she says you have no name. Your name is *Red*. The colour of smiles, and poppies and huge ripe strawberries! The colour of a door on a city street far, far away . . .'

Chapter 5

'You're very quiet,' said Bryony's mum as they made their way back to Plum Cottage. She turned to look at Bryony. 'Is everything okay?'

'Yes!' Bryony answered quickly. So quickly, she only realised afterwards that she'd just told a lie. The first lie she had ever told her mother.

Bryony immediately felt her lips go tingly. Like the lie had triggered off some fast-acting poison that was making her feel really unwell.

While her lips had gone so numb she could hardly feel them, her stomach felt like she'd swallowed a boulder! Bryony knew that she'd worry about that lie for ages.

And the truth was she was *not* okay. She'd never

been less so, in fact. If moving house had made her oddly wobbly, it was nothing compared to how Georgina had just made her feel. Georgina Brook was *cruel* to Red, who had done nothing to deserve it. He just wanted to be loved. What was so wrong with that?

'Come to the beach one day?' Bryony burst out before her mum could ask her any more questions that she didn't want to answer.

'Oh, yes!' smiled Mum. 'And maybe,' she said, 'Bella and Georgina could come too? I really did like Bella. But what did *you* think of Georgina and the pony? I bet you can't wait to go back and help with him!'

This was it. The question she'd been *dreading*. Did she do as she'd promised and make up an excuse to never go back? Or should she be honest and say she'd *love* to go back. Not for Georgina, of course – but for Red.

Bryony hesitated. *Red*. But a promise was a promise, wasn't it? And Georgina might be even nastier to him if Bryony broke the deal.

'Bryony?' said Mum.

'I'm just . . . I'm not *sure*,' Bryony mumbled, still

undecided how her answer would end. 'I mean . . . I-I thought it might be good to help with the pony – b-but Georgina is, um . . . managing. So I think that maybe . . . maybe I should just leave her to it.'

Bryony fell silent. It was done. She *wasn't* going back to Brook Dale Manor. No more Red.

'Oh!' Her mother looked really surprised and a little disappointed too. Bryony felt immediately guilty. If she had nothing more to do with Georgina, most likely Mum wouldn't see Bella much either. After Mum had just said how much she liked her.

That evening the mood inside the cottage was flat. Mum burned the fishcakes, Josh hardly said a word, and Bryony took her pony posters down. The last thing she needed were reminders of what she'd never have.

When Bryony finally wandered back downstairs, she saw Josh huddled in front of the TV with his old rugby ball in his lap. It suddenly struck her that it was Wednesday night. Back in the city Josh used to have rugby practice on a Wednesday night. Then afterwards his best mates – Max, Ollie and

Ben – would come back to their house for supper. Maybe Josh was missing his friends too, a lot more than he was letting on? Perhaps this was what this new 'gang' was all about? Josh, trying to feel like he belonged again . . .

Bryony sighed. It was all so hard! She plonked herself down beside Blueberry on the sofa. A cuddle might be nice. But Blueberry Muffin wasn't one for hugs or fussing. Besides, he was in a right strop tonight because earlier Mum had gone and confiscated the *only* mouse he'd ever caught. If he wasn't so plump (and *lazy*), thought Bryony, he might have a bit more luck! She shook her head. She may as well just go to bed.

'Sorry . . .' said Bryony, meeting her mum at the top of the wonky stairs.

'About what?' asked Mum.

'Brook Dale Manor,' replied Bryony. 'If me and Georgina had become friends, you and Bella might have too.'

Then it dawned on Bryony that her not going back would affect Mum in other ways too. The Brooks probably had tons of posh dinner parties they might have asked Mum to do the flowers for.

Their posh party friends would have seen these and maybe wanted some for their own parties. And this would have helped Mum get back on her feet *and* get to know more people too.

'Don't worry, love – I'm fine!' Mum smiled, stroking Bryony's hair. 'You sleep well. Are *you* okay?'

'Sure!' said Bryony in such an overly cheerful voice it told the *world* she was the exact opposite.

She hurried off down the landing before Mum could pick up on her sadness. Already she was missing Red desperately.

She slipped into her room and shut the door. Never before had she felt so sure that she wouldn't sleep a *wink* all night!

*

'She did *what*?!' Grandpa cried the following afternoon as he sat with Bryony in his garden.

'Why, that little madam, what a nerve!'

Bryony and Grandpa had spent the afternoon working on Grandpa's vintage car. He'd bought the car new just before he'd got married over fifty years ago. But the old MG Midget (he'd christened her

64

Matilde) had long since stopped working. In the past few years, however, after Grandma died, the old car had become Grandpa's latest 'project'.

'Well!' sniffed Grandpa. 'I hope you told your *mother* what Georgina Brook made you promise!'

Bryony was quiet.

'Bryony?' said Grandpa.

Eventually she shook her head. 'Well, no ...'

Bryony sighed, now deeply regretting that in a moment of weakness she'd gone and blabbed about Georgina to Grandpa. She hadn't meant to. It had just slipped out. Maybe because she'd had so little sleep and it was playing on her mind that Red was *there*, and would always be there without *her* ...

Looking across to the dark green MG, Bryony tried to change the subject. 'So,' she said, 'looks like *Matilde*'s almost finished.' But Grandpa was quite as determined as Bryony sometimes.

'*Why* didn't you tell her?' Grandpa went on. 'Why not tell your mum the truth about Georgina?'

'I can't,' replied Bryony. 'And *you* mustn't either. Really! It'll be fine. I just need to try and move on, I guess, and I will.'

'But Georgina Brook *blackmailed* you,' Grandpa frowned. 'She doesn't deserve that pony! I've a right mind to—'

'No, Grandpa, please!' gasped Bryony. 'Please, don't do anything – *promise me*. I don't want Mum to know the truth or she'll really worry. You should have seen her at the Manor yesterday. She seemed so happy. And I've upset her already because now she and Bella won't be friends because *I'm* not going back. And letting her know what Georgina did will only upset her more. And I just ... well, I just—' Bryony stopped.

'I just don't want Mum to be *sad*, that's all.'

Grandpa was quietly thoughtful for a moment. Then he took Bryony's hand.

'All right,' he said finally. 'I'll not say anything. But if Georgina ever bullies you again, you promise you'll tell me, yes? You're a kind soul, Bryony, and I can't bear the thought of anyone like *her* taking advantage of your good nature.'

'I promise,' said Bryony, giving him a hug. 'I'll tell you.'

Walking home that night, Bryony felt better knowing Grandpa was on her side. Not ever going

back to see Red was going to be just awful. But now, at least, she wouldn't have to pretend to be happy around Grandpa, because he'd understand.

As she emerged from the beech wood and climbed the drystone wall into her back garden, Bryony found herself in the bit she liked the most – her very own 'secret jungle'.

Here, you entered (if you *dared*) a dark, damp kingdom where monster brambles ruled and nature sent neatness packing. Here, broken flowerpots and unknown climbing shrubs greeted you from every angle: under your feet, and overhead – a thick green canopy blocking out rain and sun.

This was a place tucked away from the world. A place for remembering and dreaming up future adventures. And a place just to sit by yourself if you wanted to think.

An old garden shed hid out here too, groaning under the weight of wild honeysuckle. Next to it was an iron bench, its legs part-buried in the soil so it looked like the savage garden was swallowing it up.

This bench was a steely dark grey colour. It must have once looked beautiful, but now it was

peppered with rust. Bryony liked it all the more for that; it had character.

All around it was a sharp tangle of brambles. But Bryony could just about make out the curly metal pattern of its upright back, tendrils of dark ivy snaking round its loops and twirls.

Here was the ancient tree-swing too, hanging from one of the plum trees. The last time Bryony had swung on this she'd been bubbling over with excitement. She'd been so sure she'd find Emma again and they'd have wonderful times with Red. But of course her perfect daydream hadn't worked out.

Instead of the swing, Bryony chose today to sit on the old bench instead. Her head was as tangled up with thoughts as the bench was with rampaging ivy, so it seemed the perfect place to think things over.

Thwacking the brambles away with a stick, Bryony beat a path to its rusty seat and sat down on it beside a snail which slipped into its shell immediately.

'Yep, I get it,' Bryony sighed. The snail was as keen to be alone with *its* thoughts as *she* was with hers.

Bryony wondered why a nice girl like Emma (for Emma had seemed really nice) would choose Georgina Brook as a friend? If she ever did find Emma again, Bryony decided, she'd be sure to ask!

She also wondered how hard it would be not telling her mum about Georgina when before this she'd never had *any* secrets to keep?

And then there was Red.

However would she cope with not seeing him any more? This time yesterday – precisely now – they'd been happy in the paddock together.

'Ahhh ...' Bryony sighed. How everything could change in just a heartbeat ...

*

The next few days were horribly confusing.

Each time Bryony heard hooves on the lane she'd fly to the window half hoping to see Red, and half hoping *not* to.

Not seeing him always left her empty and sad. But if she *were* to see him, Bryony knew that not being able to run to him would be the hardest thing in the world. Not patting his face, not tickling his ears, not holding him close and feeling his heart beat. Not being able to tell him that he was *special* ...

So although it was beautifully sunny, Bryony stayed cooped up indoors. For she didn't want to risk bumping into Georgina either!

Instead she passed the time reading anything but pony stories and making models of anything but ponies. Mum asked a few times if she wanted to bake. But the last time she'd baked she'd been so excited about her visit to the Manor, and she didn't want anything to remind her of that happy night.

Then it happened, one lazy afternoon: a simple thing that changed *everything*. As a surprise, Mum baked some pastries for Bryony and left them on a plate outside her door, like they often did to cheer each other up.

Mum tapped on the door and Bryony heard her leave. Then she smelled baking and went to see. And there they were – a plate of cinnamon whirls.

'Cinnamon!' gasped Bryony. That was *Red's* special smell!

Of course, Mum hadn't realised as Bryony hadn't told her. But breathing in the smell, Bryony knew

she couldn't fight it any longer. She needed to see Red – now – or her heart would break!

'Mum!' cried Bryony, thundering downstairs.

'I—' she panted. 'I changed my mind! I'm going back ... to the Manor – now!'

'Oh, right!' Mum looked really surprised as Bryony threw on her Converse.

'Um, Josh – why don't you go too?' Mum asked. 'It'll give you something to do.'

'As if I'd want to do *that*,' scowled Josh, glancing up from his comic. 'Anyway, I'm off to meet Dartt soon. He's got his hands on some old skateboards from, err ... somewhere, and me and the others are gonna do them up.'

'From *where*?' asked Mum suspiciously. She wasn't sure about Josh's new mates.

'Anyway, see you!' Bryony called, leaving them both to it. She flew out of the door and off down the lane, her feet light and her head quite giddy. This was so out of character. So impulsive!

Georgina would be vile, of that she was sure.

But so what? She was going to see Red again, and right now that was all that mattered.

Chapter 6

Bryony's heart was in her mouth as she waited outside the Manor's smart oak door.

It opened and there stood Arabella Brook in an oyster-coloured silk dress, her shiny blonde hair in a neat and very glamorous side bun.

'Oh, Bryony!' she said. Bella was smiling but she looked a touch uncertain too.

'I've come to see the pony!' blurted out Bryony. 'A-and Georgina!' she added as an afterthought, blushing.

'Oh, dear!' Bella's face suddenly fell. 'I'm sorry, Bryony, but Georgie is poorly. Yesterday she came out in blisters and, well – it's chickenpox!'

Bryony felt her heart sink. This meant, after

plucking up the courage to come, she wouldn't be able to see Red. Not today – or probably for a whole *week*, at least.

Bella looked thoughtful. 'But if you've already *had* chickenpox,' she said, 'then by all means do come in!'

With that, Bryony noticed movement the stairs. It was Georgina, come to warn her off. She was in her nightie and plastered in calamine lotion to try and sooth her itchy blisters. She looked very sorry for herself but still managed a glower.

'Or if you *haven't* had chickenpox,' Bella went on, unaware that her daughter was eavesdropping, 'I know it's a cheek of me to ask, but maybe you wouldn't mind looking after Georgie's pony? By yourself, I mean – just until she's better? I know nothing about ponies, you see. We only bought him for Georgie because I know how she *loves* riding, and competing in gymkhanas, especially. But if you think it would be too much for you, just say . . .'

Look after Red! *By herself.* Bryony could hardly believe her luck!

Bryony had had chickenpox. But the Brooks didn't know that, did they?

Georgina was glaring at Bryony with a 'don't you DARE!' look on her face.

'I ...' gulped Bryony, crossing her fingers behind her back. Two lies in a week. What was *happening* to her! But this lie, she quickly told herself, was for Red.

'I *haven't* had it, no,' Bryony fibbed, trying her best to sound convincing. 'So ... yeah, I'd love to look after Red by myself – if that would help?'

Smiling, Bella stepped outside and closed the front door behind her. Bryony was most relieved. She was sure Georgina had been all set to storm down and *slap* her.

'To the stables, then!' Bella smiled, sweeping Bryony along. 'I'm sure Georgie will be *so* grateful!'

'Um,' mumbled Bryony, who knew full well she wouldn't. 'Yes – right!'

They arrived at the stables. And there was Red, gazing out of the stable door. Bryony knew he recognised her at once as his dark eyes widened, his ears shot up and then the left one flopped to the side. He wanted a tickle! How adorable was that! Bryony felt all warm inside, like her heart was melting.

She longed to run over and throw her arms round his neck, but she'd have to wait – just a little while longer, until Bella left.

'Now,' said Bella. 'Are you totally sure you don't mind looking after him? I'm *clueless* with ponies, as I said, but hopefully there won't be too much for you to do?'

Bryony opened her mouth to answer but Bella spoke again.

'So,' she continued, 'let me see … Georgina rides him, I do know that, and makes sure he's happy!'

At this, Bryony had to bite her lip to say nothing.

'As for all the grooming and mucking in …' Bella frowned.

'Out!' corrected Bryony. 'Mucking *out.*'

'Ah! Quite so!' Bella nodded her head. 'Well, a member of my staff does all that.'

'I–I'd like to do it *all!*' chipped in Bryony so forcefully she surprised herself.

'I mean,' she said more quietly, 'grooming is great. So relaxing, a–and according to my pony books, it helps the pony and his owner to bond. And as for mucking out … well,' Bryony

continued, 'that's all part of *having* a pony, really. Um, at least, I think so, anyway.'

She didn't want to sound like a know-it-all. But she wanted Bella to be reassured that Red would be in good hands.

'Oh!' Bella looked most surprised. 'I see! Well, if you're sure, there's some equipment to help. Come, I'll show you!'

Smiling, she led Bryony across the stable yard towards a black painted door. As they walked, Bryony glanced back over her shoulder. 'Won't be long,' she mouthed to Red – who, she heard, replied with a soft gentle nicker.

Bella opened the black door and Bryony followed her in.

'All this kit that comes with them ...' Bella shook her head. 'Completely *flummoxes* me! Shovels and bridles and saddle-y things. A whole roomful of – what's it called – tick – or, um, tock?'

'Tack!' blurted Bryony, trying to hold in a giggle. 'It's called tack.'

Bella nodded. 'It's so dreadfully complicated. Poor little pony, leave him to me and goodness – what a disaster! I mean, how often should one

feed, or bathe, or trim his nails? And arranging his hair – I mean *how*?! Why, I only know how to do my *own* because they show me at that dreadfully expensive salon I drive to every week in Nettleton! But, anyway, here are a few bits and bobs to help you exercise, groom and ride him. Do please use whatever you like!' Bella smiled.

As Bryony gazed around the tack room she saw so much equipment that looked expensive but not much used. On a nearby shelf was a grooming kit with various brushes, combs and hoof picks. And just beside that, Bryony saw a few pony books too.

Another room just next door was kitted out with the various bits to keep Red clean and fed. This included oats and hay for him to eat and some straw for his floor and bedding. Finally, there were pitchforks, brooms, shovels and a wheelbarrow for mucking out.

'Wow! This all looks great!' said Bryony.

'Really?' replied Bella. 'Well, if there's anything else you need, just ask.'

'Thanks, but there's *everything* I'll need right here!' said Bryony.

As they went back out to the yard, Bella said that

Bryony did have to make sure that her mother was happy with the arrangement too.

'Oh, Mum *will* be!' Bryony answered at once. 'I know it!'

Thanking Bryony again, Bella left. As soon as she'd gone Bryony wasted no time in racing to Red's stable and throwing her arms around the little pony's neck. How she'd missed him! Just a few days apart had seemed like *for ever.*

'I'm going to look after you, Red,' Bryony said. 'It's going to be perfect, I promise!' The pony snorted softly and nuzzled his head into her shoulder. Bryony could feel that he was excited too.

'We're going to have the *loveliest* adventures,' she smiled. 'You'll see!'

*

After a quick phone call home to check with Mum that this was okay, Bryony returned to Red's stable to get started.

She took him into the paddock right away, deciding to groom him out there. Not only was Bryony keen to get Red out in the fresh air, but here she could also start to get to know what he

liked, or what tended to spook him outside. Red had to get used to *her* too. In any new partnership you had to take things slowly and find your feet together.

It was a hot afternoon, very peaceful and calm. The grass in the paddock was soft and green. Bryony let Red graze for a bit. That way, when she started to groom him, he wouldn't be distracted by the feast right under his hooves!

When he finally stopped munching, Bryony saw both his ears slowly flop to the side. She knew that *one* ear flop from Red meant: 'Please tickle me?' But a *double* ear flop, what did *that* mean . . .?

Bryony had brought out one of Georgina's pony books she'd seen in the tack room earlier. Opening it, she looked up 'double ear flop' and discovered that ponies did this when they felt very relaxed.

'Well, that's perfect!' smiled Bryony. A relaxed Red was just what she needed as she groomed him. 'Come on then.'

Bryony kept things nice and calm as she led the little pony to the fence and tied him to it with a quick release knot. If Red *were* to get twitchy and start pulling as she groomed him, she'd be able to open this special knot quickly so he didn't hurt his neck.

'Right,' said Bryony. 'Time to get you smart!'

She began by picking out the dirt from Red's hooves with a hoof pick, nice and gently. As she did, Red stood still and calm. 'Well done!' Bryony praised him lots. 'Good boy!'

Now using a curry comb, Bryony brushed his coat in lots of little circles. This was to dislodge loose bits of hair and dirt so that later she didn't just brush over them. If not removed, these bits would irritate Red once his saddle was on – and Bryony was planning to *ride* him today too!

As she continued, Red let out a curious blow, stepping backwards as he did. Bryony guessed she was brushing him slightly differently to whoever had done it before. She stopped at once, showed him the comb and let Red give it a sniff.

'All good to carry on, then?' Bryony asked. Red bumped the rubber comb with his muzzle.

'I can? Oh, thank you!' Bryony smiled. 'Well done!'

Next she used the dandy brush to remove any dirt or loose bits of hair that the curry comb had

unearthed. Red seemed to like this hard-bristled brush as he stood very still as she did it. Bryony was beginning to realise how much this little pony liked a scratch!

As she brushed him all over in short brisk strokes, she avoided all the sensitive areas like his face, ears, tail and mane. Bryony felt so important to be the one looking after him and was determined to do her best. She'd longed for her own pony ever since she could remember and even though she knew Red *wasn't* hers, what harm could it do to pretend he was for a week or so?

Bryony finished off with a soft brush all over, even down the legs. It was amazing how Red's coat came up now – quite as shiny as a toffee apple!

When his mane and tail had been brushed too, Bryony led a *beautiful* Red back up to the stable yard and into the tack room.

'A quick lick of oil on those hooves now,' she said. 'Then we'll tack you up and go for a little hack.'

A hack! Bryony felt ever so excited. She was actually going to *ride* Red. A few days ago she'd never have even dared to dream it!

Red waited calmly as Bryony mixed the hoof oil and applied it onto his hooves with a small brush, being careful not to put on too much. The smell of the oil and the saddle leather took her back to the times when she, Fran and Becky would get the riding stable ponies ready for a gymkhana.

Bryony felt happier that afternoon than at any time since coming to Brook Dale. It suddenly struck her how lonely she had been.

Finally she got Red all tacked up. First the saddle pad, onto which she gently placed the saddle. To this she attached the girth, making sure it wasn't so tight as to pinch when he moved. As Bryony carried on getting him ready she kept talking to Red in a soft voice, telling him how very good he was being for her.

The bridle came next. Bryony always found this the hardest part. But Red accepted the bit without any fuss and stood still as she slipped the bridle over his ears. Some ponies would get all skittish. Not Red.

'Maybe you're just good for *me*,' she smiled. She'd certainly love to think so!

After a final safety check, as she'd been taught

at Park Lodge, she slipped on a pair of Georgina's riding boots, one of her hats and a body protector which all fitted really well.

'Right then, Red,' Bryony said with a smile, 'off we go!'

Bryony led Red out into the yard and was just about to mount him when she stopped.

'Butterflies!' she gasped. She had butterflies in her tummy. This was *it* – but what if something went wrong? What if Red didn't *like* being ridden? What if he got scared and threw her?

'No, don't be silly!' she told herself. Red had liked her enough to trust her from the very moment they had met. Well, now it was time for her to trust him too ...

She mounted swiftly and carefully. Best to do it decisively, she knew. Before she moved Red off, Bryony took a few moments just sitting in the saddle getting used to him. Being on a new pony's back always took a bit of adjustment.

Red was a little taller than quite a few of the ponies she'd ridden before, especially Peppermint, who'd been short and sturdy. Until now Bryony had liked Peppermint's shape but Red was far more comfortable, being smaller around the girth. Bryony's legs felt more relaxed on Red – far less like she was doing the splits! So far so good.

Bryony touched Red's flanks with her heels and he immediately started to walk on. 'Good boy!' she said in a sunny voice. 'That's the way!'

Red felt bright and springy when he walked, like he had lots of energy. So did Bryony. But where should they *go* on their very first hack . . .?

'Ah, wait!' said Bryony. 'I know *just* the place!'

Chapter 7

'Bryony!' called Grandpa from his garden gate. 'Why, I see you've made a new friend.'

Bryony beamed back as she rode Red along Grandpa's little lane. She brought him to a halt and Red gave a cheery nicker.

'Sure have, Gramps!' Bryony smiled back. 'A *great* friend!'

Grandpa stepped out to say hello to Red. He patted his muzzle and Red's eyes twinkled, clearly loving all this new attention!

Grandpa looked curious. 'But, Bryony,' he said, 'I thought you weren't going back to the Manor?'

'I wasn't,' she replied. 'Then I just couldn't bear

not seeing Red again. I haven't told Mum about Georgina, though,' she added quickly.

'I see,' Grandpa nodded. 'Well, you know what I think. But it's your decision.'

Smiling gratefully, Bryony said she had to go. She wanted Red's first hack with her to be short and sweet.

'Bye, Gramps,' beamed Bryony, setting off again.

'Have fun, and take care,' Grandpa called behind her.

'I will!'

*

This first blissful day of looking after Red was followed by more and more!

At first Bryony felt bad about leaving Mum alone (as Josh was always out with his new mates). But Mum assured her that she was fine, and said it was lovely to see Bryony so happy.

So every day, at the crack of dawn, Bryony would skip along to see Red when the sky was pale apricot and no one was about, save for rabbits and small, singing birds.

And each morning he'd greet her with a happy snort, which she'd answer with a cheery 'I hope *you* slept well too!', swiftly followed by a juicy red apple!

A breakfast of hay and oats came after that. Then she'd muck Red out, give him a quick groom, tack him up and away they'd go on their daily adventure!

These adventures started very close to home, just ambling through the fields around the Manor. And just like their first trot out to Grandpa, Bryony would keep them nice and short, as it was important to build up Red's confidence gradually.

When Red seemed fine with all of this, they went further, exploring the lanes and bridle paths dotted around the place. Finally they went on longer hacks through the woods and up the hills.

But there was one place Bryony longed to take Red just as soon as she felt that he was ready (and before Georgina got better!). And as she hurried to him one beautiful morning . . .

'Today!' said Bryony suddenly. Everything just felt right. She and Red would make that special trip today!

Bryony felt a ripple of excitement. She started to run and didn't stop until she reached Red's stable door. She opened this with a breathless 'Hello!' and Red snorted back his morning greeting. Then he clattered over and nuzzled her arm for his apple.

'Oh, Red!' panted Bryony, holding it out and waiting as he started to nibble. 'Today's adventure is the most exciting yet, so let's hurry!'

Bryony flew through her morning chores, and soon Red was all tacked up to go.

'So today, Red,' beamed Bryony, 'we're off to the *beach – hooray*!'

As she climbed into the saddle, Red replied with a whinny starting low but ending very high-pitched. This usually meant: 'What? I don't understand.'

'Don't you worry,' beamed Bryony. 'You're going to *love* it – trust me.'

Bryony had checked with Bella, and Red had never been to the beach. Best get there nice and early then, to beat the crowds.

Bryony touched Red's flanks with her heels and walked him out of the yard. They followed a long, winding path behind the house which led up and

out through the back gate. It was peaceful and not a whisper of wind. The perfect day!

The leafy lanes were pleasantly sunny as Red clip-clopped along cheerfully. They passed the allotments where an old friend of Grandpa's, Cabbage Patch Charlie, was tending to his runner beans. When he heard Red's hooves Charlie stopped and brought Red a carrot, like he'd done all week.

'Off on *another* day trip?' he asked.

'Sure are!' Bryony nodded.

'Lucky pony!' Charlie chuckled.

'Lucky *me* too!' smiled Bryony.

Trotting off down the lane, they continued until they reached some pretty fishermen's cottages not far from the beach. Bryony's grandpa lived in one of these.

'But Gramps looks still asleep, Red,' said Bryony, for most of the cottages, including her grandfather's, still had their bedroom curtains closed.

The postman, though, as usual, gave them a wave and Bryony smiled and waved back. They also saw the paper girl who always hurried past with a nod.

Bryony was starting to get known around town as the 'new girl with the cute bay pony'. And she'd never felt prouder than when showing Red off to everyone!

Grandpa's lane brought them out in a little side street just across the road from the beach.

Checking around to make sure there was no traffic coming, Bryony walked Red across the small road to the prom on the other side. This was a narrow walkway, rather like a pavement, which ran the length of the seafront. At intervals it had benches for people to sit on and watch the sea.

It also had sets of steps and sloping sandy pathways leading down onto the beach. Bryony and Red were surprised to see a group of riders coming up one of these pathways nearby.

Red greeted their ponies with a friendly nicker, and Bryony, who'd never seen him around other ponies before, was delighted to discover how friendly he was. (She might have guessed he would be as Red was so good-natured, but nonetheless it was great to see!)

The riders stopped to let their ponies say hello to Red. There were two girls; one was on a

Welsh Connemara cross and the other on a pretty palomino. There was also a boy riding a black gelding. Leading them was a lady on a large glossy chestnut horse.

'Hi!' said the lady. 'I'm Abi, an instructor up at Seaview Stables. Are you new here? Your pony's a real beauty!'

'Oh, yes!' said Bryony, feeling such a thrill to hear it. 'I'm Bryony and this is Red.' She didn't have the heart to say that Red wasn't *hers*.

'Are you coming to have lessons at our stables?' asked the girl on the palomino. She was blonde and reminded Bryony of her old friend, Becky.

Bryony hesitated.

'Oh, Alice!' said the other girl, who had long black hair. 'You shouldn't just *ask* like that.'

She looked at Bryony. 'I'm Harita – but you can call me Hari!'

'And I'm Finn,' said the boy.

'Oh, good to meet you all!' smiled Bryony.

Abi said she'd love to stay and chat but this early morning lesson had been an extra and she had to get back to the stables. They waved and headed off.

'No pressure, Bryony,' Abi smiled back, 'but

feel free to drop by the stables any time you like!'

'Um ... thanks!' replied Bryony, trying desperately to make it sound like visiting was a real possibility. Of course it wasn't. But if *only* Red *were* hers, she'd be up at Seaview Stables for lessons in a heartbeat ...

A soft nicker brought Bryony back to reality and the very special treat she'd promised Red.

'Quite right, Red!' she said. 'We're here to enjoy the seaside!' She mustn't let *anything* spoil that.

Bryony turned Red around to fully take in the scene before they went down onto the sand. There we so many new sights, and sounds, and smells! But thankfully, as it was early, the beach was still quite deserted.

The pale gold sand looked as soft as velvet and the sea was the prettiest blue. Sunlight sparkled on its surface like glitter, and above it seagulls soared through the cloudless sky.

When Red seemed relaxed with all of this, Bryony took him along to the sandy sloping pathway and began to walk him down onto the beach. But as she did she became aware of the salty breeze blowing Red's mane and little kiss curl. It

was definitely windier here than Red was used to.

Suddenly Red's ears shot back and Bryony felt him tense. With a muffled squeal he backed away and clattered to the side skittishly.

'It won't hurt you,' said Bryony, stroking his neck. 'It's just the breeze. I'll keep you safe, I promise.'

Red stopped and sniffed the air as waves tumbled and the gulls screeched out. His nostrils flared and he blew loudly, as if to say, 'What *is* this place?'

'It's the seaside, Red,' Bryony said reassuringly.

Despite her calm words of encouragement, Bryony was getting a bit worried. Maybe all this was too much too soon? Perhaps she should take him back and try again tomorrow?

She was just about to turn him back up the slope, when Red took a few tentative steps forward onto the sand.

'Oh,' said Bryony. 'You want to stay? Good boy!'

Red padded on, his hooves kicking up the sand. Later it would be burning hot, though now, Bryony imagined, it was still pleasantly cool. The tide was coming in so the waves were quite big. But there was plenty of sand between them and the sea for the moment.

When Red seemed comfortable just walking along, Bryony led him into a gentle trot. He'd trotted on lots of hacks before so Bryony figured he'd be okay with that.

At first she kept him well away from the sea, taking things nice and steady. Then, when she could see he'd got used to everything, she led him closer to the water and they trotted along the wet sand.

'That's the way!' Bryony smiled. 'Well done!'

Red was doing so beautifully, Bryony was immensely proud! Then as he trotted on, suddenly she had a thought. Should she see if Red might like to try and *canter*?

Whilst sitting in trot, she moved her right leg gently back, keeping her left leg in the normal position. Then Bryony sat up straight and asked Red to canter by giving him a small squeeze, remembering not to hold the reins too tight and to keep her back soft and supple. As Red's rhythm changed, Bryony remained sitting in the saddle, her hips free and her thighs relaxed so that she could roll with the canter. She heard the distinctive three-beat canter stride as Red's hooves hit the

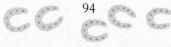

sand in stages. 'Hey, well done, Red!' Bryony called. He was doing it!

They cantered halfway along the beach. The breeze was in their faces but Red seemed to be taking everything in his stride! The sun was warm and the waves tumbled softly as Red left his hoofprints in the dark wet sand. Bryony was having the time of her life, and Red was too! The sea to their left was sweeping by in a blur – like the scenery does in a train. A beautiful blur of deep blue turquoise silk!

Then suddenly it struck Bryony that they were going really fast. She listened out for the three canter beats but now there were *four* . . .

'We're galloping!' cried Bryony, sitting forward in the saddle. 'Woohoo!'

This was the best feeling EVER. Just like they were flying! Better than that time on Peppermint, better than on any pony before! The wind was blowing Red's mane like a billowing black pirate flag, and Bryony's wild curls were streaming behind her.

She felt the warm sun on her face. Just her, and Red, and the empty beach – all of it for *just them*! The whole world was theirs and nothing could stop

them. The sea, and the gulls and Red's fast steady hooves leaving their mark in the sand. It was all that Bryony could *ever* want.

'Oh, Red,' she whispered into the wind. 'We're free!'

*

As they left the beach that day Red had a happy spring in his step and Bryony couldn't stop smiling. Next, she rode him to see Grandpa, then Mum, and they were out and about for ages! She wanted to make the most of every second they had together, because even though she tried to not think about it, it was now a whole week since she'd started looking after Red. Georgina was *bound* to be starting to feel a bit better . . .

It was late afternoon when finally they headed back to the Manor. They went in through the back gate, next to which stood a tiny cottage beside a huge ancient oak tree. On the cottage gate was a sign which read: 'Gardener's Cottage'.

Red trotted past the cottage gate, but as they neared the tree a small fluffy bundle came tumbling from it and landed with a *bump!* in their path.

'Pffffffffff!' Red let out an anxious snort, his nostrils suddenly flaring.

'It's okay,' gasped Bryony. But Red was clearly spooked. Snorting wildly again, he clattered backwards off the path, his head swinging this way and that.

'Whoa ...' called Bryony, sitting tight in the saddle in case he suddenly bolted. Red continued backwards unevenly, as if about to take an ungainly tumble.

'Steady, boy,' soothed Bryony, and it took all of her skill to steady him and turn him away from the path in an attempt to calm and distract him. She walked him forward a few paces across the grass until he regained a more even footing. Then she brought him to a halt and dismounted.

'It's okay,' breathed Bryony, patting Red reassuringly. She took a Polo mint out of her pocket and held it out to Red. He snaffled it up. Mints were great at calming him, or rewarding him every now and then. As Red was distracted sucking on the Polo, Bryony looped the reins over his head and led him to the cottage fence. She tied him to it, telling him she wouldn't be long and to

just be good for a minute. Then she hurried over
to investigate what had fallen.

The small fluffy bundle was still lying on the
path, completely motionless. Bryony looked closer.
It was a tiny baby owl!

An old wooden ladder was resting against the
tree trunk and just above it was a raggedy hole.
'Oh!' Bryony said. The baby owl must have just
fallen out of its nest in the tree.

As her gaze fell once more to the tiny ball
of fluff, Bryony suddenly caught a glimpse of
someone looking down from one of the cottage's
upstairs windows. A girl, possibly? It was difficult
to tell as she'd gone almost at once. Bryony knelt
down by the owlet for a closer look.

'Poor thing,' she whispered. It still wasn't
moving. The fall had clearly been too much for it.

As Bryony gazed down at its fuzzy white
feathers rippling in the breeze, she heard the
cottage door open and footsteps running towards
her. She turned to see a girl kneel down at her side.

Bryony went to say hello but her eyes suddenly
widened as she saw who this girl was . . .

'Emma?' Bryony gaped.

And now Emma looked puzzled too, like she didn't immediately recognise Bryony. Bryony saw Emma glance across to Red and he must have jogged her memory because . . .

'Bryony!' cried Emma. 'You've got Georgina's pony?! And I see you've met Arthur too . . .'

'Arthur?' asked Bryony.

'Yep,' Emma nodded. 'His full name's Arthur Twitt-Twoo – my little brother named him!'

Emma pointed down at the tiny still owlet, no bigger than a small round earmuff! 'Honestly, *how* many times can an owl fall out of his tree?!'

Bryony watched, open-mouthed, as Emma scooped up the little thing and cupped him tenderly in her hands.

'As I said, Will chose his name,' smiled Emma. 'And don't look so worried – he isn't – you know . . .' She lowered her voice. *'He's not dead.'*

She explained that little Arthur had fallen from his tree three times that week, and twice the week before.

'Dad said he gets hungry,' Emma nodded, 'when his mum's out hunting, and sits too near the edge of his hole.'

She pointed to the hole in the oak tree's trunk. 'Up there.'

Bryony nodded. 'So, um . . . what now?' Arthur still wasn't batting an eyelid!

'He's playing dead,' said Emma, peering closer. 'At least I *think* he is. Well, that's what he did before, anyway. Best take him inside to check him out, though. Want to come?'

Bryony nodded. 'That would be great. But first I have to take Red back to his stable. Th–that's the pony – I named him Red!' added Bryony.

Emma still looked confused as to why Bryony even *had* him, but Bryony said she'd explain it all later.

'He just needs a quick brush,' said Bryony, 'and some tea – then I'll be back!'

'Okay,' replied Emma, now cradling Arthur like a baby. 'I'll leave the cottage door open, just come on in when you're done.'

'Sure!' beamed Bryony, delighted to have found Emma again.

Bryony hurried to Red. 'Oh, Red,' she laughed, 'the flying missile, it's just an *owlet* called Arthur!'

Red's head moved up and down very quickly,

which looked just like a nod! Red often seemed like he understood what Bryony was saying.

When Red was happily back in his stable, Bryony gave him a quick rub-down, removing all traces of dried mud. Then she filled his net with hay and made sure he had plenty of fresh water.

'I'll pop back to say a proper goodnight later,' said Bryony, giving him a quick kiss on his velvety muzzle. 'See you soon!'

Closing the stable door softly, she hurried back and slipped into Gardener's Cottage through the open door.

'Oh!' said Bryony, suddenly finding herself in a small, low-ceilinged living room. How pretty it was, and so cosy! A little fire crackled in the grate, for although it was summer – and sunny earlier – the afternoon had turned chilly – as Miss Pigeon in the post office had told her could happen here ...

'Hi, come on over!' Emma called.

'Oh, thanks!' Bryony smiled back.

Emma was kneeling on the rug by the fire with Arthur flat out beside her.

'I know it doesn't *look* good,' Emma said as

Bryony knelt down too. 'But, don't worry, he's a tough little acorn is Arthur!'

'But he's . . . very still,' Bryony whispered.

'Like I said, just playing dead,' Emma nodded. 'Barn owls *do* that, you know. But when he realises he's safe he'll perk up again. Watch!'

Gently, Emma ran her finger up and down the owl's soft tummy. As Bryony watched she could *just* make out his tiny chest moving up and down. Emma was right. Arthur was definitely alive!

A few moments later, his big round eyes twitched, then opened halfway.

'Wow!' Bryony giggled softly. 'That's amazing. Hello, Arthur!'

Emma placed him in an old shoebox on a bed of dry grass. 'There we go, Arthur,' she said. 'Now let's find Dad.'

Bryony followed Emma into the kitchen with Arthur where Emma's dad was taking an apple pie from the oven, the smell of which was divine! And Will, who looked about six, was playing with his Lego.

Will looked up. 'Dad – Arthur *again*!' he giggled. 'And Emma's brought a friend too!'

Mr Lawrence turned and put the pie down to cool.

'Oh, pleased to meet you, um . . .'

'Bryony!' said Bryony.

'Oh, right!' smiled Mr Lawrence. 'And hello to you toooooo!' he said to Arthur.

Bryony grinned. 'I found him on the path.'

'Ah, I see,' Mr Lawrence replied. 'Well, jolly good!'

Emma's dad took the shoebox containing Arthur from Emma.

'Come on, then, little sausage!' he said to the owlet. 'Home you go – *again.*'

'Want to watch?' Emma asked Bryony and Bryony quickly nodded.

'Oh, yes!'

Outside, the sky was darkening as Emma's dad climbed the ladder and popped Arthur into his nest hole.

'There!' grinned Will. 'And no more falling out, Mr Twitt-Twoo!'

Mr Lawrence and Will went back into the cottage but Emma stayed outside with Bryony.

'I need to go and say goodnight to Red now,'

said Bryony, and told Emma why she was looking after him. Emma then explained that her dad was the gardener at Brook Dale Manor and that's how she knew Georgina.

'Ah! So you're not *friends*, then?' Bryony asked.

'Oh, no!' Emma shuddered. 'Just sometimes,' she said, 'Mrs Brook invites me round. Or Georgina, well . . . comes looking for me because I don't think she has, um, many friends.'

'Hmmm . . .' muttered Bryony under her breath. Why wasn't she surprised?

Emma went down to the stables with Bryony, and as they walked, Bryony was delighted to learn that Emma was ten too and would be in the same class as her at school. When they got to the stables, she introduced Red to Emma. Then, as Bryony pitchforked some fresh straw around to make sure Red's bed was nice and cosy, the little pony watched her, his eyes bright.

'He seems to adore you,' Emma said.

'Well, I adore him too!' replied Bryony. And she told Emma how much she was loving looking after him.

'Unfortunately, though,' Bryony said, 'soon it's

going to end. Chickenpox doesn't last for ever.'

'So will you still come when Georgina's well?' asked Emma.

'Yes!' Bryony answered. 'I will.'

She patted Red's head and kissed him goodnight and he let out a low, deep snort. He was happy and sleepy from their seaside adventure.

'Sleep tight, Red,' Bryony whispered softly.

Now she'd had this time with him, she couldn't imagine life without him.

Chapter 8

The next day, on her way to Red's stable, Bryony
briefly bumped into Bella.

'I'm *so* sorry to say,' Bella said dramatically, 'but
Georgie still has a few blisters!'

'Oh, no worries! I mean – how *horrible* for her
but tell her ... not to worry ... about the pony.'

Bella nodded. 'I will! And if you don't *mind*,
Red's yours for a few more days, at least?'

'I don't mind!' squeaked Bryony, desperately
holding in a cheer. 'And I hope Georgina's, um ...
not too itchy a-and scabby!'

The day had started well, and it got even better
when Emma dropped by to say hello as Bryony was
grooming Red in the paddock.

'Hi! Do you mind if I watch?' asked Emma.

'No, not at all!' smiled Bryony.

Emma said she was really nervous around ponies but wanted to get over that and learn about them.

'I really like animals and nature,' she said.

'Brilliant!' replied Bryony. 'Well, Red's the sweetest pony you'll ever meet!'

For the rest of the week (when she wasn't minding Will) Emma spent all her time with Bryony and Red. Bryony found Emma so easy to talk to, and they chatted about all sorts of things.

They took Red out for walks, and picnics too, taking it in turns to ride him. Red was such a little star! He was so calm and gentle when Emma was on his back – quite on his best behaviour. It was like he knew he needed to help her feel extra secure.

Then one warm evening, after a ride to the river, they were taking Red back to his stable, when Emma stopped near the old oak tree beside her cottage.

'Bry, do you want to know a secret?' she whispered.

'Sure!' Bryony nodded back. It felt so nice that Emma liked her enough to share a *secret* with her!

Emma pointed to a thicket of trees down the bank.

'That's a secret short cut,' Emma whispered, 'down to the orchard and stable block. It's called Pheasant Walk and only me, Will and Dad know it's there.'

'Wait, not even the *Brooks*?' Bryony asked.

'No.' Emma shook her head. 'Not even them.'

Bryony imagined how furious Georgina would be if she knew that Bryony knew something about *her* land that *she* didn't!

Emma explained that Pheasant Walk was now a wild overgrown track but used to be where lots of pheasants roosted a long time ago.

'It brings you out by a side gate near Red's stable,' she whispered.

Emma added that her dad only found out about it when he studied old maps of the land.

'Wow!' gasped Bryony. 'Can we take Red that way now?'

'It's too tangled for him,' Emma replied. 'But when Red is tucked up, you and I could come back that way?'

'Yes, please!' Bryony had always liked the wild or mysterious.

So when Red was happily in his stable for the night, Emma snuck her and Bryony into Pheasant Walk, which was everything Bryony had hoped it would be. She found herself in a magical labyrinth, so enchantingly twisted and beautifully untamed that it made the overgrown bit in her own back garden look as neat as a city park!

Emma had even made a little den from woven willow canes, moss and leaves. It looked like a fairy grotto, so cosy and snug – and so camouflaged you'd hardly know it was there!

'I hide from Georgina here sometimes,' said Emma. 'It feels doubly safe. That's why we have to keep this place secret.'

Emma looked very serious.

'Don't worry,' said Bryony. 'I won't tell a single soul.'

Bryony had her first sleepover at Emma's house that night. And as usual they chatted about all sorts. Bryony told Emma about her dad, even though talking about him was still very hard. And Emma told Bryony that her parents were divorced.

'So, did you go to your stables every day back home?' Emma asked, quickly changing the subject.

Bryony wondered if she wasn't quite ready to talk about her mum just yet.

'No, not every day – but a lot,' replied Bryony. 'Then ... Dad got sick and I stayed home more. When he used to paint, I'd make him clay models – animals, mostly. And even if the legs and heads fell off, he'd still keep them.'

They both smiled and Bryony realised that she was remembering the happy times with Dad again ...

*

The girls woke up next morning to a real scorcher. They took Red out all day exploring, right up to the top of the hills!

Then, to round off the hottest day of the year, they had an evening picnic in a beautiful wildflower meadow full of poppies, buttercups and cornflowers!

Emma had brought the food, which they ate in the tall grass – ham rolls, ripe strawberries, pasties and a yummy carrot cake (made especially for the occasion by her dad!). She'd even brought a pear and some banana skins for Red, after reading that some ponies love them!

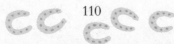

Later, as Bryony rode in through the back gate, the sky was a swirl of indigo and pink and the air was perfumed with honeysuckle.

'Wow, look at Red's coat!' Emma said suddenly, as she walked along beside them. 'It's so shiny! He looks so much perkier since you've been looking after him, Bry.'

Bryony smiled proudly. 'Thank you.' And she patted the side of Red's neck. Tonight his familiar cinnamony smell was mixed with the scent of dancing poppies and tall, swishy grass!

They carried on past Emma's little cottage and down to the stable block. But when they turned the corner into the stable yard, Bryony's heart sank. For there on the bench, eating an apple, was Georgina!

Bryony heard Emma give a little gasp, and when Red saw Georgina he stopped. Bryony had been preparing herself for this; for the day Georgina was better. But somehow, over the last few days, it had just slipped to the back of her mind. And now it was quite a shock to see Georgina back again.

'Ah, Emma,' said Georgina, her voice oddly

warm. 'I see you've made a new friend.' Her eyes shot across to Bryony. 'Thanks for looking after my pony.'

Bryony opened her mouth to reply but nothing came to her lips. This friendly-sounding Georgina was most unnerving!

'I hope you've had a good time,' said Georgina, 'and that it wasn't too much . . . trouble?'

'I . . .' Bryony dismounted, desperately holding back what felt like an *ocean* of tears. Her time alone with Red had come to an end.

Georgina smiled. Her skin was blotchy but she'd managed to avoid any pockmarks. Bryony noticed, despite the smile, her eyes were ice-cold.

'Anyway!' beamed Georgina. 'As you can see I'm quite better, so I can have my pony back.' And, taking Red's reins, she thanked Bryony again . . .

'You can go now.'

Georgina's tone made it very clear she did not expect a reply. Red was snorting nervously as Georgina held him firm, waiting.

Bryony bit her lip. It would be better for Red

if she went quickly. The last thing she wanted was for his nervousness to turn into panic and distress. But she'd definitely be back. If Georgina thought this was over, she was mistaken!

Bryony tried to leave but suddenly her legs felt as heavy as tree trunks. Every muscle of her body was willing her to stay.

Pushing through the pain, Bryony finally turned and began to walk away with Emma.

'Oh, and just one more thing,' Georgina called. '*If* you're thinking of coming back tomorrow, I should just pop along to the post office before you do.'

'H-hang on.' Bryony spun back round. 'What? Why?' But Georgina had already marched Red into the stable and she shut the door firmly behind them.

'What's she up to?' gasped Emma.

Bryony shook her head. 'I don't know but I don't like the sound of it. Meet me at the post office tomorrow morning at nine?'

'Yes!' Emma nodded nervously. 'I'll be there.'

Bryony had the sinking feeling that Georgina was at her most deadly when sickeningly sweet.

'*Ahhh* . . .' she sighed. It was going to be another long night!

*

Bryony wasn't wrong. She tossed and turned all night, unable to get a wink of sleep.

'Not wearing your jodhpurs today?' asked Mum when Bryony appeared at the bottom of the stairs in her jeans the following morning.

'N-no,' mumbled Bryony. 'I'm meeting Emma, sorry – got to go.'

Before Mum could ask any more questions, Bryony hurried through the front door. Then she ran all the way to town.

By the time she got to the post office she felt, and looked, exhausted. And Emma, who was sitting waiting on the step, looked just as bad!

'Right,' said Bryony, opening the door. 'Come on, let's get it over with.' It was time to see *exactly* what Georgina Brook was up to now.

They went inside. Miss Pigeon was nowhere to be seen so the girls started looking around. The problem was, they hadn't a clue what they were looking for.

Then Bryony stopped. In the middle of the noticeboard her eyes had been drawn to a brand new card. Bryony nudged Emma and, drawing closer, they read it . . .

Pony For Sale

A wonderful bay gelding!
Contact Georgina Brook

07798 771 225

Bryony felt numb. Like she'd just jumped into an ice-cold sea. Georgina Brook was selling Red. So anyone could buy him. Anyone except *her*. For Bryony didn't have the money. And that was that.

The numbness was slowly giving way to a stiflingly sickly dizziness. Bryony needed air. As she rushed to the door, her palms were clammy and her head was in a spin. She hurried outside into the dazzling sunlight.

Emma was right behind her. 'I'm so sorry, Bry,' she said. But all that Bryony could think about was how Red could be taken away from Brook Dale completely.

'I bet the Brooks have put ads in other places too,' said Bryony. 'Pony magazines, newspapers, online. I mean *anyone* from *anywhere* could buy him ... Georgina's won.'

'No!' Emma cried out so forcefully that it made Bryony jump.

'She ... she's such a *bully*,' Emma went on. 'I hate her!'

Bryony caught a glimpse of Emma's face. She'd suddenly gone as white as a ghost and her hands were trembling.

'Em, are you okay?' Bryony quickly asked.

Emma nodded back. 'Yes – sorry!'

She swallowed hard and Bryony waited. Something wasn't right. She knew that Emma had grown fond of Red, but this had to be something more.

'She's ... bullied me for ages,' Emma finally said, tears welling in her eyes. 'At first it wasn't ... wasn't ... too bad a–and I thought she'd get fed up and stop. But then it got worse. She started saying things about my family too. Spreading gossip about how *poor* we are and stuff – and how ... how my mum ...' Emma stopped.

Bryony nodded. Poor Emma! Bryony had only had a few weeks of Georgina but Emma had had her for *years*.

'Oh, Em,' said Bryony. 'It must have been horrible! But as for not letting Georgina win, I'm just not sure what to do. I guess I should have seen today coming. She never wanted Red in the first place.'

'But *you* do!' cried Emma. 'And Red wants *you* – anyone can see that! He trusts you and he *loves* you so much.'

'I know.' Bryony thought of those big brown eyes. 'And I love him.'

They sat down on the kerb and both fell silent, each caught up in their own memories. The street was peaceful, except for the gulls, their cries reminding Bryony of the day she and Red had run free ...

'So ... where should we start?' Emma said at last, her voice now much less shaky.

'Start?' repeated Bryony.

'Yes.' Emma looked at her. 'Start with our plan for you to get Red?'

117

Bryony shook her head. 'But how *can* I, Em? I can't buy him, we can't afford it. Besides, Mum would never agree. After the year she's had, she needs a *rest* not a pony!'

Emma nodded. 'But isn't it worth a try? Maybe start with your mum and if she *does* agree then we work out the money bit after that . . .?'

Bryony hesitated. It sounded almost impossible. But she thought of how brave Emma had been, opening up about the bullying just now. And here Emma was trying her best to support *her* . . .

For Emma then, as much as for herself, Bryony nodded. 'Okay, we can try.'

'No, repeat after me: we can *do* it,' said Emma.

'We can *do* it!' repeated Bryony. And just hearing herself say the words gave her the faintest flicker of hope. She was going to do her very best – with Emma!

They walked back, arm in arm, planning. Might as well start right away.

'I have to tell Mum everything, don't I?' asked Bryony. 'Exactly what Georgina's been like?'

'I know it'll be hard,' Emma replied. 'I mean, it's taken me so long to tell someone about her. But I did it. I just told you.'

'You mean ...' Bryony stopped. 'I'm the only one who knows?'

'Just you.'

They walked on. 'I feel better for telling you, though,' said Emma. 'So I'm sure you will too when your mum knows. And then we can plan our next move, right?'

Bryony nodded. 'Yeah. We can. Thanks, Em.'

When the girls arrived at Plum Cottage, Bryony's mum was baking ginger biscuits, and on the dresser sat a fresh vase of flowers. It suddenly struck Bryony that Mum had barely touched a flower since Dad had died. Not even the ones for Dad's funeral, although Mum had been a florist then. Clearly today was a good day for her. And now Bryony was about to ruin it by spilling the beans about Georgina!

Maybe best leave it? Bryony thought to herself. But Emma must have read her mind.

'We can *do* it,' Emma mouthed. She nodded and Bryony whispered, 'Okay.'

'Um, Mum,' said Bryony. 'Emma and me ... we've come for a chat – a–and to help!'

'Perfect,' Mum smiled. 'Just in time for the rolling. Grab some aprons!'

While Bryony plucked up the courage to tell her mum, she and Emma rolled out the biscuit dough. Bryony kept waiting for a 'good moment' but one just wasn't coming.

Finally, when the biscuits were baked (and cooled!) and everyone was sitting round the table with a pot of tea, Bryony finally decided she just had to stop putting it off.

'Mum, I've got something to tell you,' she said.

'Oh?' said Mum. 'What's that, love?'

'Well,' said Bryony, her heart starting to thud. 'The thing is ... well ... Georgina Brook ... she's not, um ... as *nice* as you think.'

'What do you mean?' Mum looked puzzled. 'You've practically lived at the Manor lately? I know you weren't sure of Georgina at first, but I thought things were fine after that? I mean, she asked you to look after her pony when she got chickenpox, didn't she?'

'No.' Bryony shook her head. 'It was Bella who asked me. *She* thought that we were getting on too. But she doesn't know what Georgina's like. And the truth is – well, Georgina's ... really mean!'

And then it all came tumbling out, about the

first day they'd visited the Manor, about the 'accident' (or not) with the biscuit tin, about the cold, curt way Georgina had spoken, and about how she'd blackmailed Bryony into *lying* in return for a little time alone with Red.

'And she's cruel to him!' Bryony cried. 'She never brushes him nicely, o-or talks to him. And she keeps him all cooped up! She never even . . .'

Bryony stopped, suddenly feeling a lump in her throat. 'She never even gave him a *name*. I did that.'

Mum opened her mouth but closed it again. She looked confused and shocked.

'But why,' she said finally, 'didn't you *tell* me all this? We never keep things from each other.'

Bryony suspected this wasn't exactly true. Mum had held back a lot of her worries when Dad had been ill, and afterwards. And Bryony hadn't spoken of her feelings of loneliness, which had only very recently started to lessen. But *now* she had a whole fresh set of worries!

'Red is for sale,' Emma chipped in quietly. 'We just saw a notice in the post office.'

'Oh.' Mum heaved a heavy sigh. 'I see.'

With that, there was tap on the door and Grandpa came in, all smiles.

'I've brought you some roses from my gard—' Grandpa stopped, seeing everyone looking so sad.

'I told Mum, Gramps,' Bryony said. 'About Georgina.'

'Wait! You *knew* about Georgina, Dad?' gasped Mum. 'And you didn't tell *me*?' She looked hurt.

'No – Mum – I made him promise *not* to!' cried Bryony. 'Because I thought that I could deal with it, and I *still* think I can because I've decided I am going to find a way to buy Red!'

'Oh, Bryony . . .' Mum went over and gave her a hug. 'The thing is, ponies cost such a lot. And I just don't have that kind of money.'

'But I didn't mean *you* should pay,' Bryony replied. 'Me and Emma! We've got a plan to get the money. O-or we will have soon!'

Mum wandered to the window and gazed out at their crazy, overgrown garden. 'And where would we *keep* him?' she asked softly. 'I just don't want you to get your hopes up, only to find it's impossible.'

'But it *isn't* impossible!' Bryony jumped up. 'What if me and Emma – I dunno . . . did odd jobs

around the place? There must be tons of people needing things done round here! That'll get us started at least!'

'They could help me,' piped up Grandpa, 'with my gardening jobs around town. My round's got a fair few clients.' At this Mum shot him a warning look and Grandpa fell silent again.

'We'd work *very* hard, Mrs May,' Emma nodded.

'Really, really hard!' promised Bryony.

Bryony looked at her mother, her eyes full of determination.

Please say yes, please say yes, she repeated in her head, her fingers tightly crossed behind her back.

'Well ... all right,' said Mum at last. 'I suppose it can't hurt to try.'

'Oh, thank you!' cried Bryony, throwing her arms around Mum. She knew this was just the *start* but knew too that you had to start somewhere!

Just then, Josh sloped in. 'What's with the hugs?' So Grandpa quickly told him the news.

'Pfff!' replied Josh with a bored-looking shrug. 'As if! Ponies cost a packet.'

'Josh ...' whispered Mum, shaking her head. 'We've just been *through* all that, thank you.'

'Hey, Bryony,' said Emma, 'we could clean windows too! We can borrow my dad's ladder.'

'Great!' said Bryony. But Josh shook his head.

'Well, sorry, sis – you can count me out, too busy!'

Bryony frowned. He didn't *look* sorry as he happily tucked into the biscuits. She and Josh used to be really close, but in the last couple of weeks she'd hardly seen him. And, when she did, he was always so edgy.

'When's lunch?' demanded Josh, scowling at Mum. 'I'm meant to be meeting Dartt again soon. Got any crisps or sausage rolls?'

'Oh, Josh,' Mum sighed. 'No, I haven't. You'll stay and have a proper lunch for once.'

Well, *Bryony* wasn't staying with her brother like this. Making an excuse that they needed to get the ladder, she quickly headed off with Emma. Josh didn't care about anything any more.

Except for Dan Artt and 'the others' . . .

Chapter 9

The plan to buy Red began that very afternoon with cleaning a ton of dusty windows!

Emma helped too and for the rest of the week the girls hardly stopped. This was good as it kept Bryony busy, although the little pony was never far away from her thoughts.

As well as window-cleaning, they washed cars, painted fences and walked countless dogs. They also helped Grandpa and Emma's dad with their gardening, and Miss Pigeon even took the girls around town helping her to deliver groceries.

They were on one of these trips at the end of the week, heading off to visit a Miss Parsley (or

so the name on the grocery box said), when the subject of the summer fête came up.

Until that day Bryony had heard nothing of this annual fête but as they walked to Miss Parsley's, Miss Pigeon could talk of nothing else! Today was Friday and the fête was a week on Saturday, she informed them.

'August the eighteenth to be precise!' she said. 'Two o'clock 'til five – come rain or shine, mind you!'

Miss Pigeon then stopped to talk to a passer-by about the cream teas for the fête. And while she nattered on, Bryony asked Emma a little bit more about it.

'So, do you have stalls and competitions?' said Bryony.

Emma's finger shot to her lips.

'Not so loud,' she whispered. 'Competitions and Miss Pigeon equals trouble. Double trouble, if you throw in Miss Parsley too!'

Bryony was very curious to find out what she meant, so Emma took her aside to make sure Miss Pigeon didn't hear . . .

Miss Dorothea Parsley and Miss Eliza Pigeon, Emma said, had attended the summer fête ever

since they were little girls, and that was over seventy-five years ago. And for all that time the pair had been the fiercest rivals!

According to Emma, both old ladies loved entering the various fête competitions. And Emma said they both loved *winning* them too. So much so, they spent nearly all year planning and plotting their entries.

'And their *favourite* competition,' warned Emma, 'is jam. So under NO circumstances mention – you know what.' She mouthed the letters: 'J-a-m.'

Bryony giggled. 'It can't be that bad!'

'It is.'

Upon their arrival at Miss Parsley's tiny pink cottage (right next to Miss Pigeon's tiny blue one), Miss Parsley welcomed the girls with a cheery 'Good day!' She nodded curtly at Miss Pigeon and Miss Pigeon nodded curtly back. Bryony could see what Emma meant. Already you could cut the tension with a knife.

Dorothea Parsley was short and round. She had lots of frizzy, silver-grey hair and cheeks the colour of two scoops of strawberry sorbet, which was also the colour of her cottage. She couldn't have looked

more different to the bony, neat-bunned Miss Eliza Pigeon, whose sharp violet-blue eyes were the colour of *her* cottage!

The girls were fascinated by Miss Parsley's place. Bryony had not been in any of the oldest-looking cottages just behind the town's main street, and although Emma had peeped inside from Miss Parsley's doorstep when carol singing at Christmas, she'd not been inside the cottage either, until now ...

Bryony looked around, eyes wide. This was enchantingly spooky! It was dark and small, and the walls were so thick it felt like they were in a cave. More like a *cavern*, Bryony thought, as pots and pans bubbled with rainbow-coloured liquids, all thick and gloopy and smelling of fruity potions.

'Do you think she's a *witch*?' Bryony whispered to Emma as they stood beneath ceiling beams adorned with swathes of dried hops and bunches of dusty lavender and rose hips.

'Probably,' Emma whispered back. 'But I don't *think* she'll turn us into frogs,' she added, grinning.

As well as owning various black cats, and making super-fruity jam, Miss Dorothea Parsley always

took it upon herself to make posters advertising the annual summer and Christmas fetes.

These posters she painstakingly painted in watercolour, and when she whipped them out to show the girls, Bryony thought they did look rather beautiful with their summer flowers and lazy bees along the top and sides.

'You're a very good artist,' Bryony said to Miss Parsley, at which Miss Pigeon bristled and sniffed. Emma shook her head quickly so only Bryony saw. Bryony bit her lip. She'd need to be more careful what she said!

'I need 'em putting up now,' Miss Parsley smiled. 'Fancy it, girls? I could pay you a little bit of pocket money.'

'Oh, yes!' Bryony said at once, eager to earn whatever money they could to buy Red.

'What yous entering at the fête then?' Miss Pigeon sniffed, eyeing up Miss Parsley haughtily.

'You doin' *jam*?' Miss Pigeon prompted, at which Bryony gave a gasp. Jam! That was the *one* thing that Emma had said sent the old ladies into all-out WAR!

'Might be!' snapped Miss Parsley, bobbing her

head in the direction of the stove where numerous pans blooped and rattled. 'Ah, but I thought you would *know*, Eliza – as you're *meant* to be able to tell the future! Huh!'

Frowning back, Miss Pigeon stuck her nose in the air. 'Well, I *do*,' she said. 'I just ... sometimes pretend I DON'T as I don't like boasting 'bout me WONDERFUL TALENT!'

'Rubbish!' cried Miss Parsley. 'Poppycock! You daft old fibber you!'

'I ain't no fibber!' Miss Pigeon roared. 'You old bullfrog!'

As the two old ladies rolled up their sleeves, Bryony shot a nervous look at Emma.

'Better watch out!' Emma whispered. 'Like I said, when they get on the subject of the summer fête they're *brutal*!'

Sure enough, there was moment of brooding silence as both old ladies eyed each other menacingly. Who would make the first move? Bryony would have bet *anything* (except Red!) that Miss Pigeon would be the one to go in first.

But no.

Suddenly Miss Parsley gave a snort and advanced

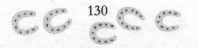

like a raging tornado. Snatching up an egg from the egg box just delivered, she hurled it through the air in the direction of Miss Pigeon, who whacked it away with a baguette.

'Time to leave,' whispered Emma.

'Yep,' whispered Bryony. '*Quick!*'

The girls ducked outside with the posters, and when they were safely on the street . . .

'I see what you mean!' Bryony giggled. 'Brutal!'

They started to stick the posters up. They had about twenty of them in all.

'Hang on, Miss Parsley's used *watercolours*,' said Bryony as she pinned one up in the bus shelter. 'So won't the paint wash away in the rain?'

'Yep!' Emma nodded. 'Always does! But everyone knows when and where the fête is. It's the same time, same place every year.'

Bryony read down the poster, as she *didn't* know.

'Oh, right, Brook Dale Manor. *Of course* . . .' she groaned. 'Best house for miles, right?'

'And Georgina *loves* it,' Emma frowned. 'Strutting about like she *owns* the place – which . . . she does!'

Both girls found this surprisingly funny, when a

few weeks ago *neither* would have. But being a team, united against Georgina, and with a plan too, seemed to be making things a little easier for them both.

At the same time Bryony never lost focus. All these jobs were for money to buy Red. And the faster they worked, the more money they'd earn – simple!

'Come on,' she said. 'Let's get these posters up quickly. Then we can help Grandpa with more gardening.'

'Okay,' Emma nodded. 'Good idea!'

They arrived at the park and Bryony started to pin a poster to the noticeboard really carefully. All week she'd taken great care over all the little jobs she'd done. If people were paying her good money, she'd hate to do anything half-heartedly and disappoint anyone.

But as she was about to put in the last pin, Bryony stopped and spun round.

'Emma! These fête competitions!' she cried. 'If you win, do you get any money?'

The posters were advertising all sorts of things from pet shows to scarecrow-making and photography.

'Sure,' replied Emma. 'They pay really well if you place first, second or third.'

'So let's enter as many as we can!' said Bryony. 'The more money we win, the—'

'More money to buy Red!' Emma finished her sentence with a nod.

'Yes, exactly,' Bryony said. 'This is great!'

They only had just over a week to get all their entries ready. And they'd have to be good or they wouldn't stand a chance. Not if the two old Miss Ps were anything to go by!

Turning back round, Bryony was beaming as she popped the last pin into the poster, when all of a sudden, out of the blue—

Wham!

Something cold, hard and splattery had hit her on the back of the head. It had also covered the poster in messy brown splodges.

'OW!' Bryony yelled. 'That really hurt!' She rubbed her head and frowned.

'Mud!' cried Emma. Solid clods of it, and lots of soft smelly mud too. Both girls turned just in time to spy a rowdy gang clearing off down the road.

'Oi!' Bryony called after them. But suddenly she

went very quiet. The gang were on skateboards, wearing hoodies with the hoods up. Even then Bryony could pick him out. The one skating slightly behind all the others, with the skinny white freckly legs. It was her *brother*. Josh had pelted her with mud. How – why? Why was he *being* like this?

'Dan Artt's gang,' Emma sighed. 'Dartt's at school with me. And he'll be in your class too. He's a right pain. And his gang are as well.'

'Oh, *Josh* . . .' groaned Bryony, shaking her head and spraying mud everywhere. Just *what* had her brother got himself into?

*

The next day was Saturday. One week before the fête. The girls met early at Plum Cottage to start on their competition entries.

'*Eeek*,' gulped Bryony, 'there's tons to do, and we haven't got very long.' They'd have to be organised. There wasn't a moment to lose.

The first thing they did was put up a tent in the back garden. This, they decided, would be their 'Crafting Headquarters'.

Josh stuck in his head as he set off to meet his little gang of 'mudslingers'. He didn't stay long, though, disappearing promptly when Bryony completely ignored him. They'd had a big argument last night after what had happened in the park. And Bryony was in a no better mood with him today.

The girls checked down the list of competitions they were going to have a go at – the Cakes for Afternoon Tea class, the painting class, the photography class entitled *Reflections*, the Make-a-Scarecrow class, the Home-made Jam class and the Miniature Flower Arrangement class.

'I know it's a lot,' Bryony said. 'But the more we enter, the more chance we have of winning at least *something*.'

All of Saturday was taken up with painting a picture for the painting class. The subject was 'The Journey', and whilst Bryony painted the journey of a butterfly in and out of the flowers, Emma did the journey of a snail. Except her snail just wanted to stay in its shell and do nothing!

After that, they took photos of reflections in the rock pools at the beach for the photography class.

'I think we've done well today,' said Bryony as they looked at their work that night.

'Yes!' Emma nodded back brightly. 'Me too!'

On Sunday the girls decided to make jam, so they went blackberry-picking bright and early. They knew the Miss Ps would be hard to beat but the twenty-pounds first prize meant that they had to try!

When countless bowls and jars were crammed full of berries, Bryony's mum insisted she supervised the cooking of the fruit. It was likely to get blisteringly hot as the berries bubbled and slowly mushed down into jam.

By Sunday evening, umpteen jam jars brimmed with deep purple loveliness! There was even some blackberry jam left over for Bryony and Emma to have with scones as they camped in the tent that night.

'It's been a good day,' Bryony said. 'If only Red had been with us – he would have really loved the blackberries.'

'I know,' nodded Emma. 'But we're doing it to get him, yes?'

'Yes.' Bryony forced herself to smile. 'You're right.'

Both girls were brown from the warm August sun and their faces were smeared with berry juice. As they continued to nibble through their midnight feast, they talked about all kinds of things: school and friends, and ponies, of course – Emma was definitely warming to them thanks to the time she'd spent with Red. When she grew up, Emma wanted to be a vet, so becoming more familiar with ponies would be very useful.

'You know so much about the countryside,' said Bryony. That had been clear when the girls had been blackberry-picking.

'I'm on the nature team at my school,' replied Emma. 'I mean *our* school,' she corrected.

'Oh, yes!' said Bryony. Then she had a thought.

'Wait! Does *Georgina* go there too?'

'No, don't worry,' Emma replied. 'She goes to a posh school a few towns away.'

'Phew!'

When the owls were hooting madly and a huge moon hung in the sky, Bryony's mum brought out mugs of hot chocolate with marshmallows floating on the top. As the girls drank them, Bryony couldn't help her thoughts turning, once again, to Red.

She had always loved settling him down at night, tickling him behind his left ear the way he liked just before she said goodnight. She wondered if anyone would be doing that now? By anyone, of course, that meant Georgina. Bryony doubted he'd be getting any hugs or tickles from *her* . . .

The hot chocolate soon made the girls sleepy so they snuggled down in their sleeping bags. The tent was slightly see-through and Bryony could *just* make out the stars. Small, silver, sparkly balls, they were dotted all about. Like the owls had decorated the sky with strings of fairy lights!

'My mum used to like camping,' said Emma sleepily. She'd said hardly anything about her mum before, only that she was no longer with her dad.

'Do you still . . .' Bryony stopped.

'Go on,' said Emma.

'I was just wondering if you . . . if you still see her sometimes?' said Bryony. 'But you don't have to say if it's hard.'

'It's okay,' replied Emma. 'Mum . . . moved to France when I was eight, and now she has a boyfriend who's got other children.'

'It must be really hard,' Bryony said.

'Mmm. But I've still got Dad,' replied Emma. 'And Will, and now there's *you* too.'

'Yes!' said Bryony. That felt nice to hear.

'Night, Bry,' yawned Emma.

'Night, Em.'

*

On Monday the kitchen was a hive of activity as the girls got started on their cakes for the Afternoon Tea competition. They chose to make eclairs, the cakey bits of which they'd bake now and then freeze until Friday. This would keep them really fresh. And making them early meant if they went wrong, they'd have time to do another batch. On Saturday morning they'd fill them with cream and a sweet plum compote. Then they'd finish them off with a shiny chocolate glaze.

Tuesday was scarecrow-making day. Emma thought they should make a 'different' kind of scarecrow though because *everyone*, she said, made normal ones. Finally they decided that their scare*crow* would be – a massive *crow*! Its body would be made from bent wire coat hangers, which would then be covered with copious amounts of black crêpe paper and feathers!

This, however, proved very tricky and so took up much of Wednesday too. They were very glad when just after tea, Bryony's grandfather dropped by with a bag of sherbet lemons he'd just bought for them at the shop.

'Crafters need to keep their energy up!' he chuckled, peeping into their HQ. 'But – oh, my!' he cried. 'Aren't you doing well?' And rolling up his sleeves, he helped them stick a few last feathers on their crow.

'If you win it'll be down to that last row of tail feathers!' Grandpa said with a chuckle.

'Okay,' nodded Bryony, and Emma gave a grin. 'For sure!'

Thursday was miniature flower arrangement day. The theme was 'The Secret Garden' and Bryony and Emma had decided to do a display based around a drystone wall. Except miniature meant that everything had to be tiny.

They made the wall from smooth flat pebbles they'd collected off the beach last Saturday. Into this they wove the daintiest trails of ivy and

honeysuckle they could find. They finished it off by threading in tiny flowers.

Finally, on Friday (they'd put it off as long as they could!) it was time to spruce up Blueberry Muffin for the fête's pet show.

'Hold him still!' cried Bryony.

'I'm trying!' Emma giggled. 'Come back, Mr Grumps, and have your bath!'

The plump grey cat was growling loudly and his fluffy (unwashed) tail was swishing about. A sure sign to keep well away!

At long last, with water everywhere and several new scratches on their hands, they finally bundled him into the tub brimming with sweet-smelling bubbles.

'*Meowwwwwww!*' The cat was angrier than ever, splashing, and yowling wildly.

'I don't think he's keen on Mr Fluffy's cat shampoo,' said Bryony, dodging the claws.

'Me neither!' said Emma. 'Let's wash him quick and get him out!'

They only managed a few bubbly swishes before Blueberry was climbing up the sides. Emma scooped him out onto a nice warm towel and wrapped it around him quickly. Now he looked like a cross fluffy baby in a shawl!

When dry, he was combed. But the cantankerous moggy didn't seem to like *that* either. To top it all off, on his collar Bryony tried out a big lilac bow to see if he should wear it tomorrow. Berry looked revolted, his face like thunder and his fur smelling like a rose.

'Who's a pretty pussykins, then!' Bryony giggled as Blueberry scowled.

Well, that was it! The girls were all done. Apart from their eclairs still to decorate in the morning, their week of crafting was over!

That night, they chose to sleep inside the cottage as their HQ was full of their creations. Before bed, though, Bryony was *still* thinking money. What else could she do to earn extra pennies for Red?

She looked in her wardrobe. At the bottom of it were two boxes filled with old toys. She hadn't had the heart to part company with these when she'd moved here just a few weeks ago. Just a few *weeks*! It felt like much longer given all that had happened.

'Right, these can all be sold!' Bryony said, businesslike.

'Are you sure?' asked Emma.

'Yep,' Bryony nodded. Suddenly toys didn't compare to a living, breathing animal!

As well as the toys, there were various clay models Bryony had made as she'd worked beside her dad. She shook her head. She couldn't part with these. Besides, she told herself, they probably wouldn't sell, being a lot more precious to *her* than to anyone else.

Next Bryony rifled through her jewellery box to see if there was anything else in there she could sell. She pulled out a rainbow tangle of bracelets and bangles.

'Hmm, most of these can go,' she said. '*If* we can ever untangle them!'

'I'm good at untangling,' Emma replied. Bryony wasn't surprised. Quiet and careful, Emma was by far the more patient.

The girls dug deeper into the jewellery box. There were lots of pretty rings and hair clips too. Bryony still liked most of them, but right now she didn't mind selling them for Red.

Emma then unearthed a black velvet pouch tied with a pale blue ribbon.

'Not that!' cried Bryony. She hadn't meant to

shout but what was in that pouch was *very* precious.

'Oh, sorry!' gasped Emma. She passed it to Bryony, who undid the ribbon and carefully tipped out a small silver locket, which sparkled brightly in the palm of her hand.

Bryony opened the locket and, deep in thought, gazed at the contents for a moment. Then she turned it around for Emma to see too.

'My dad,' said Bryony, pointing to a picture on one side of the opened-out heart. The opposite heart had a tiny lock of hair safely encased behind the glass. Bryony remembered Dad's curls, the same shade as hers. And his hair had been every bit as unruly too.

When she next spoke, Bryony's voice was quiet.

'This is my biggest treasure,' she said. 'I wear it when I need good luck.'

'Will you wear it tomorrow to the fête?' asked Emma.

'Yes. I've never needed *more* luck than I will tomorrow.'

Carefully nestling the locket back away, Bryony slipped the pouch under her pillow. It was getting late, so the girls got into their pyjamas and settled

down for the night, Bryony in her bed and Emma in a sleeping bag on the floor beside it.

As Bryony closed her eyes, she felt nervous but excited. Tomorrow was a very big day. She had to sell and sell and *sell* to even be in with the smallest chance of affording Red ...

Hours later, as Emma snored softly, Bryony was still tossing and turning. Something had only just occurred to her. Something that made her feel sick.

As well as the usual locals, the fête would bring in *other* people too – lots of visitors from outside. All the more to discover that 'Pony For Sale!' ad in the post office.

It would only take *one* of them to decide to buy Red, and Bryony's dream would be over ...

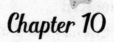

Chapter 10

Mum dropped the girls off at Gardener's Cottage an hour before the fête was due to start. The Brooks had stipulated that no one was allowed to 'jam up their front drive with vehicles', saying that instead they must park on the lane outside the Manor and unload their cars from there.

Bryony's mum had intended to do that until Emma's dad had pointed out that *he* lived on that land too, and she was more than welcome to stop at his cottage for the girls to unload.

They had arrived in plenty of time to display all their competition entries, and set out their stall nice and neatly. Bryony longed to nip and see Red first. She'd been missing him so much! And

he was so close, yet it felt like he was a million miles away.

'Do you think I could just say hello?' she asked Mum. 'Just for *one* minute – I'd be quick!'

Mum shook her head. 'Best not, love,' she said. 'Just stick to the plan, stay focused and try to stay calm around Georgina.'

Bryony sighed. Mum was probably right. 'I know,' she said. 'I just *really, really* miss him!'

Mum stayed by the car to look after the cat as the girls unloaded their boxes of sale goods and took them along to their stall.

'Smart kitty!' cooed Mum and Blueberry glared. Behind his very sweet-smelling right ear (and making it constantly twitch!) was the huge lilac bow, firmly back in place after yesterday's dress rehearsal.

'I do hope he cheers up, though,' grumbled Bryony as she and Emma headed off.

'I'm sure he will!' Emma replied optimistically.

They followed the pathway down from the cottage which brought them out on the Manor's smooth back lawns.

'*Wow* ...' gasped Bryony. Emma's dad had worked so hard. The lawns, freshly mown, looked

as smooth as velvet. And the shrubs and flowers were at their very best – not a twig, not a petal out of place. He'd had Will to look after all week too, more than happy for Emma to off go and help Bryony with the competitions.

'The locals do love the fête,' Emma said. 'And as you can see, they also like to *decorate* . . .'

There was handmade bunting draped from tree to tree, and there were neat bunches of balloons everywhere!

The girls unpacked their bits to sell and arranged them neatly on their stall. As they did, Bryony noticed some familiar villagers setting up their stalls and games too.

Abi, the riding instructor from Seaview Stables, was running the coconut shy. Next door was the Fish-a-Dish-Hoop-La stall run by Saul Salmon the fishmonger. Emma said if you hooped five or more rubber fish standing upright in little yellow buckets, you'd win a *free* fish supper in a pretty pottery dish.

There was also a traditional skittle ally run by someone Bryony didn't know (yet!). And in the centre of the games a striped wooden helter-skelter

twirled up into the cloudless blue sky, and Cabbage Patch Charlie stood ready to man the mats.

Further down the lawns were two huge white marquees surrounded by a huddle of smaller ones. They reminded Bryony of a flock of snow-white swans!

'One of those bigger marquees,' explained Emma, 'is the competition tent. It's where our entries will be displayed and judged, and where the pet show happens too.'

'And the other one?' asked Bryony.

'Oh, that's the food tent,' replied Emma.

Outside it Bryony saw a couple of girls she'd met from Seaview Stables the day she'd taken Red to the beach.

'Hi!' Alice called, and Bryony remembered that she rode the pretty palomino. And the other girl, Hari, who had been on the Welsh Connemara cross, waved.

'Hi!' Bryony waved back to them, smiling. But even as she did she thought again of Red. He'd love to be friends with their ponies if only he were hers ...

'Oh, and see that *coloured* marquee?' Emma said. 'Now *that's* for Mademoiselle Oiseau!'

She led Bryony towards the only marquee that wasn't white, but a mysterious teal blue. It was painted all over with little gold stars and on the top fluttered a pale purple flag. A large sign in the shape of a crystal ball stood just outside its entrance. It was entwined with ivy and Bryony read it:

Mademoiselle Oiseau sees ALL. Find out your future for just £1.75!!

(And no freebies this time if she told you things last time that haven't happened – YET!)

'Mademoiselle Oiseau?' said Bryony. 'Hang on a minute, doesn't "Oiseau" mean "bird" in French?'

'Yep!' grinned Emma. 'That's Miss *Pigeon's* fortune-telling tent!'

Bryony grinned too. 'Do you think she makes them up? Her "all-seeing" predictions, I mean.'

'Well ...' replied Emma thoughtfully. 'She does get *some* things right. Like she predicted at the Christmas *Eve* fête that it would snow on Christmas Day – and it did!'

Emma, Bryony saw, looked rather impressed. But Bryony couldn't help thinking that Mademoiselle Oiseau only had to check the *weather forecast* to have known that!

The smaller marquees had various crafty things for sale, or demonstrations of woodturning, weaving or pottery. There was certainly going to be lots going on.

Now that the girls' stall was set up, they hurried back to the car to get their competition entries. Then they took them along together to the judging marquee.

Inside it was ever so busy, with serious-looking people putting out their things and secretly eyeing up the competition.

Bryony and Emma started to set out their entries, and arrange them as neatly as they could. Each item had a card with a number on too and a description of what they had made.

As Bryony was popping the final card on

151

their scare-*crow*, she spotted Georgina Brook. Bryony bristled, but it was bound to happen sooner or later.

Georgina was setting out her 'Afternoon Tea' entry but she was not alone. Fussing round her were three girls, all in expensive-looking clothes. Bryony pointed them out to Emma.

'They're from her posh school,' Emma whispered. 'Not friends. Just girls who hang on to her on fête day because it's at her house.'

Georgina must *love* hangers-on, thought Bryony. She seemed really comfortable playing the princess and lording it over them. She was pointing, and seemed to be telling them *exactly* how her cakes were to be displayed.

With that, Georgina spotted Bryony too, and her lips curled into a smirk.

'Oh, look!' called Georgina. 'It's Little Miss Too POOR to Buy a Pony of her Own!'

'Well, at least I'm not a—'

'Bryony ...' Emma whispered nervously. 'Remember what your mum said. Stay calm ...'

'Fine.' Bryony took a big, deep breath, willing herself not to be riled. But the fête hadn't even

started yet and already Georgina knew *just* how to wind her up!

They carried on arranging their competition things. Then Bryony gave their crow one final fluff up as it sat beside a *brilliant* traditional-looking scarecrow in dungarees and a big straw hat.

'All done, then!' said Emma, whisking Bryony back outside.

Bryony was still fuming about Georgina but the phrase that kept going round in her head was *pony of her own.*

Georgina's words had made Bryony want to see Red more than *ever.* Maybe she could nip there now? But then ...

'Time to get Berry!' Emma said, starting off across the grass. 'Come on, Bry,'

'Okay,' sighed Bryony. 'But I hope Mr Grumpkins is in a better mood, that's all!'

Back at Gardener's Cottage, Bryony's mum was talking to Emma's dad out in the sunny garden. She was pointing at his beautiful hollyhocks lining the crooked path when suddenly it struck Bryony that both of them had *flowers* in common. She briefly wondered if he might know of a shop that Mum

could maybe rent in town. If and when, of course, she felt ready . . .

Will was with them too, wearing a most unusual costume. It consisted of huge green crêpe-paper leaves Will had used his handspan as a template for. On his head was a bright red bobble hat, with other red bobbles sellotaped along his leafy arms.

The girls, who were going to be busy on their stall, weren't entering the fancy dress. Will had offered to do that for them, and give any prize money he might win to Bryony.

'He's meant to be a giant tomato plant!' whispered Emma. 'Just in case you were wondering, Bry.'

'Ah . . .' smiled Bryony. 'I can see it now! Hey, Will!' she called over as they reached the garden gate. 'I really like your costume!'

'Thanks!' Will cried, flashing a big gappy smile.

Bryony thought Emma's little brother was great, and her dad was too. Mr Lawrence had sandy yellow hair and was very calm and kind. And although the Brooks kept him terribly busy, he always made time for everyone.

Bryony would *hate* being gardener here as the place always had to look 'perfect'. Emma had told

Bryony during one of their sleepovers that Arabella Brook, though very polite, was also very particular. If she had her way Emma's dad would be working day and night!

As for Austin Brook, Georgina's father, he was a lawyer and worked away a fair bit. When he *was* home, though, according to Emma, he was mostly snappy and didn't like to be disturbed.

Bryony suspected that the Brooks didn't pay Mr Lawrence that much either. She knew that Gardener's Cottage came free with the job, and wouldn't be surprised if the Brooks thought that this was enough! Emma didn't seem to have many different outfits but Mr Lawrence had noticeably fewer. He mostly wore old linen shirts and blue faded trousers. And occasionally he was seen in a threadbare olive-coloured jacket.

'Mum, where's Berry?' Bryony suddenly asked. They'd left him in his carry-case in the shade of the oak tree but it had now disappeared off the grass.

'Oh, no!' gasped Bryony, suddenly remembering little Arthur. Berry was a *devil* for not exactly *chasing* birds (as he was too lazy to chase anything), but he was very good at lying in wait and *then* he

155

had a mean left hook! She quickly scanned the ground for stray feathers and any other evidence of a scrap.

'Don't worry, Bry!' said Mum. 'Mr Lawrence took Berry into the cottage to stay cool. And we gave him some cream – which he loved!'

Bryony breathed a sigh of relief. 'Phew!'

Mr Lawrence went to get him. 'There you go,' he said, passing the carry-case back to Bryony.

She checked. Berry was snoring loudly, blobs of cream, like hailstones, dotted round his whiskers – greedy guts!

The pets were judged as soon as the fête opened. Then Mum and the other pet owners could take their little darlings home. The last thing the Brooks wanted was a riot in their spotless garden!

Bryony walked with Emma and Will to the stall, then carried on with Berry to the judging tent. On her way, however, she couldn't resist taking a *really* quick detour to the stables. Just one tiny peep at Red was all she wanted. Just a peep!

They were almost there when, out of the blue, Berry started to yowl most unhelpfully.

'Shhh!' hissed Bryony. Did he have to do that

now? What was making him cry out like this? Then she remembered. Cream! It occasionally made his tummy a bit dodgy. Mum must have forgotten.

'Oh, dear, you'll be okay, though,' Bryony whispered. 'But, *please, shush.*'

Scowling, Berry turned his back on her, but at least the yowling stopped. Bryony carried on, rounding the corner into the stables. The yard wasn't empty, so she ducked back out and peeped around the wall instead.

'Grrr!' Bryony huffed under her breath. Georgina Brook and her school posse were there, laughing and pointing into Red's stable. Bryony could just make out his beautiful ears. They were flat back, which meant he wasn't happy.

'Useless!' Bryony heard Georgina scoff and guessed at once she was talking about Red. How *dare* she!

Bryony retreated – slowly, and most reluctantly, willing Berry *not* to yowl. But luckily no one had seen them come or go.

Just then, the village clock struck two. The pet show would be starting any second!

'Quick!' gulped Bryony. She'd have to be fast

or Berry would be disqualified! She belted back to the judging marquee, arriving *just* as they were closing the tent flaps.

'S-sorry!' panted Bryony, slipping inside. 'Just in time!'

She made her way carefully across the tent, carry-case held high. Random pet dogs were running wild, chasing their tails, or in the case of two pugs – each other! A twitchy sheepdog was attempting to round them up. And a frog on the loose was croaking very loudly, pursued by three boys with a jam jar!

In his allocated space along a vast trestle table, Bryony swiftly unloaded Berry onto a neat velvet cushion and propped his show-card in front of it. She'd written his details in her very best handwriting ...

> Blueberry Muffin.
> Friendly(ish) Grey Cat.
>
> Hobbies: sleeping, eating, and clawing furniture (occasionally).
> Dislikes: bubble baths, rain, some people – but not everyone.

'Now, please do try to look *elegant*,' she whispered to the grumpy cat.

The judge was a lady in a smart country jacket who wore a badge saying:

Mrs Honeywell
Head Judge

She marched along the line like a sergeant major, examining the pets one by one. Most of them, Bryony thought, were actually a little bit dull. Timid guinea pigs, sleepy hamsters, and the odd stick insect (which Bryony suspected were just *sticks*!). And Jed Jenkins, the farmer's grandson, had brought along a billy goat that did nothing but *nibble*! It particularly seemed to like the judge's pencil . . .

'No!' barked Mrs Honeywell. 'Jed Jenkins, kindly stop – um . . . does the goat even have a *name*?'

'Goaty McGoatface,' answered Jed, nodding.

'Well!' Mrs Honeywell gave a rather sniffy tut. 'Stop him chewing!'

Finally she halted at Blueberry Muffin who, to Bryony's surprise, was sitting aloof and tall. His coat was soft, and he still (just about) smelled of Mr Fluffy's cat shampoo. Thankfully too, he hadn't yet ripped off his bow.

Berry let the judge examine him with a glare but no nasty swipes.

'Very twinkly eyes!' Mrs Honeywell noted.

Then, when things were going so well, Berry started to hack. And, throwing back his head – '*Caaaacchhh!*' – coughed out a lumpy grey thing!

It landed – *SMACK* – between the judge's eyes and she reeled back, slightly dazed. Time seemed to stand still for a moment now as Bryony willed her *not* to tumble. 'Don't fall … don't fall …' she chanted desperately under her breath.

But it was no good, for …

'Argggh!' cried Mrs Honeywell, the goat-nibbled pencil flying from her grip. The clipboard went after it, then countless bits of paper – flapping about like crazy white doves! Bryony closed her eyes, hoping that when she reopened them, things would be back to normal.

But no.

Mrs Honeywell was now flat on the floor under a mountain of paper.

'Th-that CAT!' she spluttered. 'The little horror – it *spits*!'

'No!' Bryony cried. 'That's a *furball*!'

She could feel her ears burning.

'He didn't *mean* to,' blushed Bryony. 'It must have been the cream that brought the furball up! *I'm so sorry*!!'

Bryony could feel hundreds of eyes now fixed squarely on *her*. She spotted Georgina, who couldn't have looked more delighted!

'Kindly take your cat and his ... *furball* home!' Mrs Honeywell now hissed at Bryony. She was peering, cross-eyed, at the hairy grey *lump* still stuck to the bridge of her nose.

'And could *someone* pass me a wet wipe or SOMETHING!' she bellowed.

Wishing the ground would swallow her up, Bryony bunged Berry into his carry-case and fled outside, back to her mother.

'How—' began Mum. But Bryony was in *no* mood for questions! Dumping a very disgruntled Blueberry, she turned on her heel and disappeared off back to Emma on the stall.

'So—'

'Don't even ask, Em!!' Bryony puffed, still red and completely mortified.

'Oh, dear,' gulped Emma quietly.

'*Yep,*' Bryony groaned.

But the *good* thing, Bryony now saw, was that their stall was very busy. The girls had been cunning with their pricing and it looked to be working too. They had priced a few key things very cheaply to get the crowds hooked in, so that they'd be tempted with things that were a *lot* more expensive.

They both proved excellent sellers too, and were – for quite a while – flat out! Finally, when it got a tiny bit quieter, Emma slipped off and returned with two ice creams.

She passed one to Bryony.

'*Thanks!!*' Bryony cried.

'It's only an ice cream!' grinned Emma.

'No, not for the ice cream,' Bryony smiled. 'Although strawberry does happen to be my favourite! No, I meant for everything you've done since I got here.'

Bryony was really grateful to Emma, who had nothing to gain from all this. Emma was such a

good friend, someone she could count on. Not like *Josh*.

Across the grass, Bryony could see her brother's new gang making their way to the coconut shy. Dan Artt was in front – obviously – in his on-trend black hoodie and trainers. And for the fête he'd done his hair in a stupid gelled-up quiff!

Dartt was the master of swagger. Skulking in the shadows wasn't for *him*. No, that was the job of 'the others', who were sloping just behind. There were three of them, built like gorillas, with deep thunderous glares on their faces. Finally, bringing up the rear, was her brother. He was walking a step or two behind the others like he didn't quite fit in. And he looked more like a meerkat than a gorilla, being much weedier than the rest. Occasionally he appeared to forget to 'slope' too, but then he'd remember and quickly jump back in line.

Bryony hadn't the foggiest idea why Josh would hang out with these boys. She'd once wondered if he was missing his old rugby friends and was trying to use Dartt's gang to replace them. Or had *she* been too busy recently looking after Red to hang about with her brother like she used to?

Bryony couldn't bear the thought that she'd driven her brother to this gang. For it was clear, even to her (after only being around a few weeks), that things always seemed to happen, or go missing, whenever Dan Artt was about. Smashed windows, broken fences, swings torn off their hinges were often left in his wake. Of course, though, it was *never* Dan. He always seemed to have an excuse. Why dirty *his* hands when he had minions, like Josh, to do his dirty work *for* him?

'How much for that?'

'HEY!' came a voice. 'How much for *that*, I said!'

'What?' Bryony was jerked back to reality by the cold sharp glare of Georgina. She was flanked by her schoolmates, all glaring at Bryony too.

'That locket!' Georgina pointed.

'N-no, that's—' stuttered Emma.

'I'm not talking to *you*!' snapped Georgina.

Bryony's hand shot to the locket catching the sun around her neck. The locket that held her dad close to her heart . . .

'It's not for sale,' Bryony answered flatly, matching Georgina's glare.

'Ooooooooooh!' heckled Georgina's well-dressed posse.

'It is if I *say* so!' snapped Georgina. Her white-blonde hair was shimmering and her porcelain face quite perfect. She stood there like one of the tall white foxgloves, beautiful but deadly.

'Give it to me!'

Chapter 11

Bryony stepped back. Then gathering herself, stepped forward again. She didn't want Georgina to sense how nervous she felt.

They stood like an untouched game of chess. Firm and square, waiting for battle.

'I won't,' said Bryony. 'It's my locket. And some things are not for sale.'

'Huh!' Georgina shouted. 'Then I'll *take* it!'

Before Bryony could dodge away, Georgina shoved Bryony's hand off the locket and ripped it clean off her neck.

'You—' Bryony lunged at her, yelling wildly. But her cries were drowned out by the

uproarious laughter coming from Georgina's little gang.

The table was in the way, blocking Bryony from Georgina and the locket, which was now firmly in Georgina's grip. With a smirk of victory, Georgina turned to leave. But suddenly something came flying through the air and – *splat!!*

Bryony blinked, trying to take in the scene. Georgina had stopped in her tracks and her beautiful blonde hair, which a moment ago had hung down her back like shimmering silk, was splattered in green ice cream with small brown sprinkles.

'M-mint choc chip!' Emma stuttered nervously, just about standing her ground.

Finally she'd managed to summon the courage to stand up to Georgina. But Emma had gone very pale and was shaking wildly.

'How DARE—' In the moment the ice cream had hit, Georgina – in shock – had dropped the locket which had landed on the grass near the stall. Bryony flew to snatch it up, but another hand just beat her to it.

'Here, Bry.' Josh stood back up and passed the

locket to his sister. 'And I'll make sure we'll fix the catch as well, don't worry.'

'Oi! What you *doing*?' came a furious voice, and Dartt marched up, seething. He'd been watching the action from the coconut shy with his three thuggish mates.

'Why stop a good fight – you *loser*?!' Dartt spat, punching Josh hard on the shoulder.

'What *is* it, anyway?' Dartt looked at the locket glistening in Bryony's palm.

'Silver,' he smirked. He held out a beefy hand. 'Let's have it, then.'

Bryony's fingers snapped around the locket.

'*I* had it first!' Georgina rounded on Dartt.

'Yeah?' glowered Dartt.

'Yes!' thundered Georgina. 'And this is *my* land so what I say goes!'

As Dartt and Georgina weighed each other up, Dartt clicked his fingers, glancing at Josh. 'The locket – get it – now!'

Bryony's eyes met her brother's. What was he going to do? Side with Dartt and get off without bruises, or side with Bryony and make an enemy of Dan Artt?

'*That*,' answered Josh, looking squarely at Dartt, 'belongs to *my sister*, and no one else.'

'Enough!' Georgina cried, her nose in the air. 'I demand that, that ... you *leave* my property. Or I'll have you thrown out, ALL of you!'

Bryony could see people starting to look across. Dartt suddenly seemed aware of them too and shuffled, looking a bit shifty.

'Huh! Who wants to stay, *anyway*?' he snarled, barging Georgina out of the way.

'And *you!*' Dartt spun round to look at Josh now. '*Traitor. You'll be sorry.*'

Dartt marched off, and a second later Georgina flounced away too. She smelled strongly of mint and left a trail of sticky drips behind her.

The three girls from her school suddenly looked most relieved to be finally rid of her.

'Okay, helter-skelter time!' beamed one. 'Now *she's* gone we can do as we like!' And turning around, they skipped off giggling brightly.

Bryony slipped the locket into her jeans' pocket.

'D-do you think Georgina *will* get us thrown out?' Emma asked nervously.

'No,' replied Bryony. 'You live here too. But

I expect that, after she washes her hair, there'll be payback.'

Josh was quiet. He caught Bryony's eye and put the hood of his sweatshirt down.

'About these last few weeks,' he mumbled. 'I didn't mean . . . it was just . . . well, sorry.'

'It's okay,' said Bryony. 'I know it's been hard. Starting in a new place, and leaving everyone behind and missing, well . . .' Bryony stopped and bit her lip.

'Dad,' said Josh softly. 'Yeah, you're right. It has.'

The stall had got noticeably quieter now, probably because of the argument. Josh offered to mind it for a bit if the girls wanted to have a break. Emma was keen to go and watch Will in the fancy dress parade at four o'clock and asked Bryony if she wanted to go too.

'Um, you go on and I'll find you in a bit,' replied Bryony, slightly distracted. In the distance she'd just spotted a fluttering purple flag.

'Hmm,' she muttered under her breath. 'I wonder . . .'

*

'Ahh, you came!' said a cheery voice trying to sound deep and mystical. ''Course, I *knew* you would!' Mademoiselle Oiseau grinned. 'Come – sit!'

The fortune-telling tent was humid and dark, and it smelled of the post office in town. That was because the post office and this tent had one thing in common – Miss Pigeon!

Bryony battled through a maze of net curtains to the centre of the mystical labyrinth. And there, on a deep green velvet armchair sat Miss Pigeon, dressed up as Mademoiselle Oiseau.

Her fortune-telling clothes were really over the top. And Bryony, despite her current flat mood, found – to her surprise – that she now had to hold in a giggle.

Miss Pigeon was wearing a long, curly black wig with a sequinned shawl tied around her head. She had big, hooped earrings in her wrinkled ears and wore dozens of bracelets which jangled every time she moved.

On the low table in front of her sat a large crystal ball. Beside it was a small flowery teapot and an assortment of mismatched bone china teacups and saucers.

Bryony knelt down on a squashy purple floor-cushion and paid her one pound seventy-five. The tent, she noticed, was lit with a number of battery-operated candles and tea lights. When Mademoiselle Oiseau saw her looking at them she shook her mystical head.

'Huh! Real ones aren't allowed,' she huffed crossly. 'Health and safety!'

Bryony suddenly wondered why she'd come in at all. It wasn't as if she *believed* that Miss Pigeon could actually *see* the future. It was simply because she felt so desperate to know what would happen to Red. Right now it felt like it was all so up in the air . . .

'Right! Tea leaves for you!' Mademoiselle Oiseau beamed.

'S-sorry?' replied Bryony, puzzled.

Mademoiselle Oiseau didn't reply. Instead she picked up her flowery teapot and poured out Bryony a cup of tea in a yellow china cup which sat upon a pale pink saucer.

'Here – drink!' said Mademoiselle Oiseau, sliding the teacup to Bryony. 'But mind you leave some tea at the bottom,' she added. 'And don't

slurp up the *tea leaves* neither as we'll be needing 'em, see?'

Bryony nodded, although she didn't *see* at all. This was all quite curious and odd. The tea was lukewarm and not very nice, but Bryony managed to drink most of it down.

'Um, Mademoiselle Oiseau,' Bryony said, 'I was wondering if my future, kind of, involved a new ... *animal* coming into my life?'

Bryony didn't want to give too much away. Rather, she wanted to see if Miss Pigeon could actually work things out for herself. Making it too easy for the 'Lady of Mystery' would mean that Bryony wouldn't know whether to *believe* her or not!

Mademoiselle Oiseau pointed to the teacup still in Bryony's hand.

'Well – swill it round, then, dear!' the old lady said. 'Then tip the tea leaves out on your saucer.'

With another nod, Bryony followed her instructions.

Mademoiselle Oiseau explained that Bryony's tea leaves would reveal *pictures* that would help her predict Bryony's future.

Bryony couldn't see how. All *she* could see was a soggy brown lump that looked like a large crusty scab!

'Ahhh,' said Mademoiselle Oiseau, peering in closer. 'Very, very interesting! What sort of animal are you hoping for, dear?'

'Well, there's this—' Bryony stopped herself. 'What do *you* see, Mademoiselle Oiseau?' she asked.

Flicking back her fake curls, Mademoiselle Oiseau looked annoyed but returned her gaze to the tea leaves. After prodding them round with her spoon a bit, she looked suddenly rather excited.

'Ahhh!' she cried cheerily. 'The mist is clearing. I see an animal with four legs ... and a neck!'

Bryony looked around. There *was* no mist. Not even in the crystal ball!

'And?' said Bryony, trying not to sound impatient. Quite a few animals had four legs and a neck. Bryony had been hoping for something a little more *specific*.

'And – wait! It has a *face*!' cried the old lady brightly. 'It's becoming clearer and clearer. Yes – now then, my dear, how would you feel about ... a *tortoise*?'

'A t-tortoise?' Bryony frowned. 'Well, I do like

tortoises but I like *other* animals quite a bit more.'

'Well, lucky for *you*, then,' Mademoiselle sniffed, 'it AIN'T a tortoise I see in your future!' Blowing her nose, she looked again.

'A rabbit? No – wait! It's bigger than a rabbit but ... smaller than a giraffe. Oh yes! I see it now – why, it's a little pony!'

'A pony!!' cried Bryony. 'And ... and – is he mine? O-or does he belong to someone else?'

'He certainly *loves* you,' the old lady answered. 'And I see that you love him too.'

'But ... !' cried Bryony. 'Is he *mine*, do you think?'

'It's tricky, my dear.' The old lady shook her head. 'I see trouble ahead but you must follow your heart! I see water – and a car and—' Suddenly she stopped, for Bryony was now on her feet.

'S-sorry!' stuttered Bryony. She should never have come. And trouble ahead! She certainly hadn't wanted to hear *that*.

'I'm sorry – I must go!' Bryony cried, turning and running from the tent. She was even more confused than she'd been before she'd stepped inside it!

Outside, the afternoon sun dazzled her eyes. She rubbed them, staggering round the back of

the tent for some shade to try and think straight. What now? Where now? What, if any, should her *next* move be ...?

And then she saw it. And her heart missed a beat. Georgina Brook had returned with nice clean hair and a thoroughly *rotten* plan to go with it!

Payback.

Yes, this was it! But it was much worse than anything Bryony could have imagined.

For there on the grass, just behind the marquees, was Red – freed from his prison to give *pony rides*. Georgina Brook was determined that everyone would *see* him, in the hope that someone might buy him – here and now!

Around his neck Bryony saw a freshly painted sign ...

Pony
for sale

RIGHT NOW!

Red looked so sad. Bryony could hardly bear it! His head was bent low, his ears flat back and his beautiful rich coat had lost its shimmer. His little kiss curl was still there, though. And those beautiful ears that loved to be tickled. And the star. The little star in between his eyes!

Suddenly Bryony couldn't see for tears, which she let tumble fast and free. Red – he wasn't hers, and if Georgina had her way, he never would be!

'No, please ...' Bryony's words were barely a whisper. She willed herself not to give up. She would go. Go and count the money she'd earned. She *couldn't* let Red slip away. She'd *beg* Georgina to let her buy him if that's what it took.

Bryony spun round to race back to her stall, and bumped into a boy.

'S-sorry!' she gasped. But the boy seemed distracted, and was looking over her shoulder ...

'Hey, is that your pony?' he called.

Bryony turned to see Georgina nod back.

'Yes!' she smiled. 'Come and see him before someone *else* buys him, quick!'

The boy ran over and Bryony trailed behind. Her legs had gone to jelly.

'Hi! I'm Jonathan,' the boy said to Georgina. 'I've been looking for a bay gelding for ages. Does he jump well?'

'Like a *dream*!' Georgina beamed. 'In fact I'm ever so sad to be selling him, but—'

'You can't!' Bryony heard herself shout. 'You can't sell him to this boy!'

'Says who?' snapped Georgina, her pale eyes icy. 'He's *my* pony and I'll sell him to whoever I like!'

Georgina turned to lead the boy away but Red had other ideas. As Georgina pulled his lead rein, he clattered back wilfully, snorting and flinging back his head to look at Bryony.

Bryony made towards him, then Georgina pulled harder and Red was dragged off behind them.

'Right, Jonathan,' Bryony heard Georgina say. 'Get your parents and we'll do the deal now!'

'I c-can't,' answered the boy. 'I'm not from around here. I've been up staying with my uncle for a week and my parents don't collect me until tomorrow.'

'Bother!' cried Georgina, and Bryony could hear that her normal angry tone had returned.

'I could phone Mum and Dad tonight?' said

Jonathan, his voice getting quieter the further away they went.

'I could ask ... bring the trailer,' Bryony heard him say. Then his voice finally faded to nothing.

'The trailer!' cried Bryony desperately. Red was as good as sold. That was it. There was nothing she could do now.

When Bryony wandered back to the stall, Josh and Emma looked really pleased. Will was there too. He'd won the fancy dress and held out his prize money to Bryony.

'I ...' Bryony stopped. 'I d-don't feel very well. I need to go home I think – sorry!'

'Oh, no!' Emma gasped. 'Shall I pack up what's left?' There were only a few bits and bobs.

'Thanks,' answered Bryony, hurrying away.

'Bry!' called Josh.

'Stay with Emma!' replied Bryony. 'I'm going home to bed. I'll see you later!'

A few hours later, Josh tiptoed in, but Bryony was pretending to be asleep.

'Bry,' he whispered, putting down a tub of money on Bryony's bedside table.

'We made loads of cash. I'll leave it here. You can count it in the morning, maybe? Your flower garden thingy got second place. Then Miss Pigeon won the jam competition and all *war* broke out when Miss Parsley hurled this dodgy *crow* thing at her. Coat hangers and crêpe paper everywhere, there was. Nightmare.'

Chapter 12

'How much have you got, then?' Grandpa asked, when Bryony had finished counting.

'£237.61,' Bryony said with a sigh. She put down her pencil and Grandpa opened the car door and sat down on the driver's seat beside her.

'Bryony, I could always stay,' he said kindly.

'It's okay,' replied Bryony. 'Honestly, Grandpa. I sort of always knew I'd never make enough money to buy Red anyway. And after yesterday and that Jonathan boy, I don't know why I even bothered counting it! Georgina would never sell Red to *me* . . .'

Bryony had told Grandpa everything as he'd been cleaning his old car. *Matilde* now sparkled and her engine purred softly. She was clearly back to her beautiful self.

Storm clouds were gathering in the sky as they sat on Grandpa's driveway. It seemed yesterday's fête had stolen Sunday's share of sunshine too.

Bryony tipped the money back into her rucksack. There'd be no more talk of Georgina.

'Your car looks wonderful, Gramps!' she said, forcing herself to smile.

'Thank you, pumpkin,' Grandpa replied quietly.

Bryony was determined not to spoil the day. Her grandfather had been waiting for this Sunday for ages. He was off to a vintage MG Midget show in Nettleton, a few miles north of Brook Dale. He'd been to this show every year since Bryony could remember. But every single time in the past he'd admired other people's cars. Today he finally got to show off his own.

They went inside and Grandpa made a flask of coffee for the journey. As he screwed the lid onto his old thermos flask, Josh came in through the door.

'We can do better than that, Gramps!' he said, putting down a big picnic basket.

'Me and Mum made you some lunch. Take a look!'

'Thanks, Josh!' smiled Grandpa, opening the lid and taking a peep inside. 'Oh, cheese and pork pies and lemon cake – my favourites!'

'You okay, Bry?' Josh had noticed his sister, sitting in the window seat quietly.

'Yeah ...' replied Bryony. She still hadn't told him about yesterday. 'Let's get you into the car, Gramps,' she said. 'You don't want to be late for the show.'

'If you're sure you don't need company today?' Grandpa asked.

'Why?' asked Josh. 'I'll be about, but what's wrong?'

Grandpa nodded at Bryony and Bryony nodded back. Josh deserved to know the truth. And so, as Grandpa packed the car, Bryony told her brother everything.

'So, anyway – I don't stand a chance now,' she concluded. 'Jonathan's parents are coming today, and they're bringing their horse trailer too. Jonathan seemed to think that Red was just what he's been looking for.'

No sooner had Bryony finished her story than

her brother whipped a crumpled paper bag from his pocket.

'For you,' said Josh. 'I-I brought it in case you hadn't made quite enough money. It's well, it's all my money from Patrick.'

Patrick was Josh's piggy bank. Josh, Bryony knew, wasn't great at saving, but she was so touched that he'd give her everything he had.

'Thanks, Josh,' said Bryony. 'But this is yours. And even if we offered Georgina *the crown jewels* she wouldn't sell Red to me.'

'I bet she would!' nodded Josh. 'Have it anyway – 'cos ... well, I just *want* you to.'

Bryony smiled.

'Right, then ...' said Josh. 'That's that.'

It was almost ten o'clock, time for Grandpa to go. The twins went out to wave him off.

'Have a great time,' Bryony said.

'Rev her up, then, Gramps!' called Josh. Grandpa turned the key and *Matilde* started, her engine purring majestically.

'Bye!' Grandpa called, and he tootled off down the lane *just* as the rain started.

Bryony decided to go and see Emma. She really

ought to tell her how much they'd made. And now that she definitely couldn't buy Red she'd insist she share the money with Emma. It was the least she could do after Emma had been such a great friend.

Josh went with her. Yesterday he'd promised Will that he'd help him make a go-kart in the garden. By the time they got there, though, the rain was already much heavier.

'I'm so sorry, Bryony,' Emma said when Bryony had told her the news about Red. 'Is that why you left the fête early?'

'Yep,' Bryony nodded.

For the next few hours, Bryony paced around, waiting for the sound of a trailer. Josh tried to talk her into helping with the go-kart they were having to build in the kitchen.

'I can't,' she said. 'I just wouldn't be able to concentrate.'

Lunchtime came and went. Still no sound of a trailer. And Bryony was more anxious than ever. Then, finally . . .

'I need to see Red!' she cried. 'One last time, to say goodbye! I can't have him think I've forgotten him and that I don't care.'

Her mind was made up, and no one could stop her. 'Well, go down Pheasant Walk,' suggested Emma. 'That way you won't be seen.'

'Pheasant Walk? What's that?' asked Josh.

'Em!' shouted Will. '*You told Bryony the secret?*'

Emma nodded. 'She's my best friend, Will.' Then they shared the secret with Josh too.

'Whoa,' said Josh. 'A secret short cut wilderness? That's ... that's really cool!'

'Don't tell anyone, though,' Emma said and Josh promised that he wouldn't.

The others said that they'd go with Bryony. But Bryony wanted to be alone with Red to say her last goodbye and persuaded them to wait for her at the cottage.

'Right, then,' she said, borrowing one of Emma's raincoats. 'Won't be long.'

As she set off down the overgrown track, Bryony knew this was the last time she'd ever see Red. No more taking him big red apples, or exploring Brook Dale together, or watching the world flash by as they galloped along the sand.

She stumbled through the soaking wet brambles, whacking them away with a stick. Why did bad

things always happen to *her*? Why did Georgina hate her so much? Why did she *ever* think things could work out fine?!

Bryony emerged from the secret labyrinth by the side gate near the stables. But suddenly she stopped. For there by the gate was ... Georgina!

Thank goodness, though, Georgina hadn't seen her. If she could just sneak back into the thicket and wait until Georgina went away, then she could carry on with her plan to see Red.

Georgina was looking up at the stormy sky as she leaned against the open gate. The rain had just stopped but was threatening to return any second.

Bryony started to edge back towards the trees. But she stepped on a twig which snapped loudly, promptly giving her away.

'Hey!' called Georgina, her face puzzled. 'Where have you just *appeared* from? And why are you *here*, anyway?'

'I ...' Bryony stopped. 'I just wanted ...' she gulped.

'Ah, yes,' Georgina nodded. 'Of course, I should have known! You just wanted to bid farewell to the *sad little pony*.'

Her tone was mocking and a teasing smirk danced around her dainty lips. 'Pity, then, because you're a *tiny* bit too late!'

'What do you mean I'm too late?' Bryony gasped. Georgina just stood there and laughed.

Bryony rushed to the stables. Red's door was open wide but Red was nowhere in sight.

'*Where is he?*' she screamed. Bryony didn't understand. Had Jonathan and his parents taken him already? Perhaps they'd come and gone through the side gate? Is that why she hadn't heard a trailer go past Emma's?

But wait – all Red's tack and blankets were still there. Even his favourite tug-and-toss-ball was hanging up on his peg.

Bryony shook her head. This just wasn't making sense! She flew back to Georgina.

'*Where's Red?*'

'Oh, dear,' smirked Georgina. 'I'd tell you if I could. But as you can see someone's been careless and – oops! – left the gate open. If a little pony were to wander through, why, who *knows* where he might end up? I do hope he hasn't come to any ... harm.'

'What?' shrieked Bryony. She glanced at the open gate. 'You! You let him *out!*'

The world was spinning and Bryony was boiling hot, yet her hands felt cold and clammy.

Turning, she raced back to Gardener's Cottage, but this time up the bramble-free driveway.

'Emma!' she shouted. 'Josh – *quick!* Georgina's let Red wander out! Come on – we have to go and find him – now!'

'She's done *what?!*' cried Emma, horrified. She too had become very close to Red, spending all that time with him and Bryony.

'Right, best search close to home first,' Emma said. 'Then gradually work outwards. But my dad – he's out. I can't leave Will!'

'Great!' cried Will. 'I'll come too!' Being only six, this was like a huge adventure.

'As long as you do as I say,' warned Emma.

'Okay!'

By the time they reached the side gate Georgina had gone. Then the sky gave a thunderous rumble.

'That's *not* a bad omen,' Bryony whispered to herself.

If *only* she believed her own words . . .

189

Chapter 13

They started their search in the fields around the Manor then fanned out to the meadows beyond.

It had started to rain heavily again and the sky was growing darker all the time. Clearly a huge storm was approaching, and there was still no sign of Red.

'Okay, where else might he go?' asked Josh as they regrouped on a soaking wet lane, looking like drowned rats.

'Anywhere!' cried Bryony. She was starting to feel frantic.

'No, wait!' she gasped. 'Red loved the *beach*!' She remembered that special trip they'd made back when Georgina had chickenpox.

'Right,' said Emma. 'Let's go there next, come on!'

They set off, running as fast as they could. The quickest way from where they were was through the beech wood. As they headed there Bryony could only imagine how wild the sea would be today. Emma, it seemed, was thinking the much same . . .

'Will – no going near the waves,' she called. He was such a little daredevil at times.

Will frowned. 'I'm not a *baby*, Em!'

'I know!' called Emma. 'But it's going to be rough and really dangerous!'

Emma, who'd lived in Brook Dale all her life, knew the tides like the back of her hand.

'Okay, so it's three o'clock now,' she panted. 'We'll have until four before the tide will be too high for us to search the beach any more.'

'Oh, no!' cried Bryony. That was hardly any time at all!

As they approached the beech wood, Bryony saw her little cottage. There was no time to call in and tell Mum what was up. They couldn't waste a single second. The advancing tide wasn't going to wait until their search was done. If Red was at the beach they needed to get to him fast!

Inside the wood the leafy green canopy acted like a huge umbrella, allowing them to pick up more speed.

Everyone sprinted through the wet ferns and piled out of the wood, breathless. They were nearly there, just a lane or two to go.

They ran on until they reached the sandy pathway leading down onto the beach.

'The *waves*,' cried Bryony. 'Look at them! They're fierce!'

The sea, now dark grey, was wildly rocking about. In the distance Bryony could see the boats in the harbour. Usually they were in neat little rows but today they were bumping and crashing into each other, pulling against the ropes tying them to the jetty and threatening to rip themselves free. The waves were huge too, hissing and spitting and *unstoppable*.

Thankfully the tide was still a little way out so they hurried down the pathway onto the sand. As they searched round the sand dunes, the sky looked dark and menacing. Then Bryony saw, in the corner of her eye, a single flash of silvery lightning. She herself had never been scared of thunder, but she knew that Red *hated* storms. Especially wind, and now it was blowing a gale!

'Maybe,' she cried above the roar of the sea, 'he's gone to shelter in a cave?'

'Yes,' gasped Emma. 'Yes, you might be right.'

Some of the caves were clearly too small but others would easily fit a pony. And a few of them looked deep and cavernous.

'Right,' said Josh. 'Let's search them quickly!'

Bryony checked her watch.

'Three-forty,' she said. 'Just twenty minutes left until the sea floods the caves completely! I think we should split into pairs to save time.'

Emma chose Will (to keep an eye on him) and Bryony went with Josh.

'Meet back here at five to four!' Bryony called behind her.

It was very gloomy inside the caves, worse than usual because of the storm.

'Red! Red!' they called through the darkness, but the only answer they got was their own ghostly echo: *'Red! Red!'*

Bryony could hear the sea crashing outside and each time they changed caves the waves were closer than before. The storm was showing no sign of letting up either.

Bryony thought she spotted Red once or twice but the shadows were clearly playing tricks on her eyes as each time it turned out to just be rocks. They had barely a few minutes in each of the caves if they wanted to get them all checked in time.

Those fifteen minutes passed in a flash, and before they knew it, it was time to meet back up.

They had one more cave to search. The one closest to the steps. And the sea was coming faster than they'd thought.

'There's no time,' said Josh. 'We've only got five minutes. That last cave – look, it's *huge*.'

'But *Red* . . .' Bryony gasped. What if he *was* in there? Waiting. Scared. Alone . . .?

Deep down, though, she knew that Josh was right. Even now the sea had reached their feet, the freezing salty water biting cold. Then suddenly something caught Bryony's eye. Will was racing off towards the cave!

'No, Will!' she yelled.

'STOP!' Emma shouted. 'There's no time!'

Will was at the mouth of the cave. He heard

them though he still ran on inside. Everyone chased after him. Will's intentions were good but the sea was marching closer all the time.

They piled into the cave. 'There!' Josh pointed. He could just make Will out, running further into the damp, eerie darkness.

'Red! Red! Where *are* you?' Will called.

'*Will!*' wailed Emma.

'Come back!' called Bryony. But as she raced towards him she didn't see a rock lying in her path on the ground. She flew past it, but as she did, a jagged bit sticking out cut through the skin on her ankle.

'*Arghhhhh!*' screamed Bryony, tumbling to the ground, her ankle stinging like mad.

'Bry!' called Josh, hurrying over with Emma. And Will, who'd also heard, rushed back.

'Bry! Are you okay?' gasped Josh.

'Oh, Bryony, how bad is it?' asked Emma.

'*Sorry ...*' said Will quietly. 'I only wanted to find Red.'

'It's o-okay,' shivered Bryony. It was too dark to see how deep the cut was but she felt blood trickling onto her foot.

'Listen, I'm f-fine!' Bryony said. 'But we've g-got to get out of here – *now*.'

They helped her up, and as they went to head out, a surge of freezing water came at them.

'The sea! It's *inside!*' Bryony shouted. '*Brace yourselves!*'

The wave hit and then they waded through numbingly cold water as the sea gulped and gurgled around them. Bryony winced as the salt stung her ankle. She pushed on, but it was hard fighting against the waves. As hard, thought Bryony, as the battle to get Red away from the cold-hearted Georgina. Like fighting against the tide – Bryony didn't stand a chance. She never had!

Suddenly she felt cold to the bone and sick, and the echoey cave started to spin.

'*Dizzy* …' she gasped. Josh held her tight, helping her through the icy water until all four of them were outside. As they staggered up the pathway leading off the beach they looked back to see the last patch of sand disappear in a surge of ice-cold water.

'Red,' whispered Bryony.

There was nowhere he could shelter. Not now …

Chapter 14

The rain was finally stopping as they walked back through the beech wood. Bryony was still thinking about Red.

'I miss him so much,' she murmured to Emma.

'I know,' replied Emma. 'But if you can, try to not think the worst.'

They walked on a little further when . . .

'Bryony! Josh!' It was their mum, with Grandpa back from his car show.

'Where have you been?!' cried Mum rushing over, Grandpa hurrying behind. 'Me and Grandpa – we've been looking for you for *ages*.'

Before anyone could answer, Mum hugged them. Then she noticed the cut on Bryony's ankle.

'Bryony, what happened to your foot?' she cried. But Bryony's mind was not on herself.

'She c-cut it on a r-rock,' Emma shivered.

There was seaweed on their clothes. Grandpa noticed it too.

'Don't tell me you've been in the caves?' he said. 'It's not safe in high tide, and you know it!'

Josh, Emma and Will all looked really sheepish, but Bryony was still distraught.

'It was *her*,' she said, gulping back a sob. 'Georgina Brook sent Red out and now he's *never* coming back!'

'Never coming back?' Grandpa repeated. 'But we *saw* Red just ten minutes ago.'

'You what? You *saw* him? Where?!' gasped Bryony. She could hardly believe what she was hearing!

'At Brook Dale Manor,' Grandpa answered. 'We went to see if you were at Emma's and then – well, we saw him there.'

'By the way, Emma,' Mum now said, 'your dad's very worried too. He's gone off to the park to search while we searched here in the wood.'

'I'll go and tell him I found them,' Grandpa

nodded. He turned to leave but Bryony stopped him.

'Grandpa – but *Red*! Was he okay?'

'As right as rain!' Grandpa replied. 'He was coming back in through the side gate with Seth Davies.'

Seth Davies was the farrier who fitted Red's shoes, or trimmed his hooves when they needed it.

'I think Mrs Brook must have "summoned" Seth,' said Grandpa, 'to take Red in to get new shoes. When *I* saw them Seth was in his Land Rover, pulling Red's trailer behind. He was bringing the little pony back, like I said, ten minutes ago.'

Bryony now breathed a huge sigh of relief. 'Thank goodness!' she cried. 'Red is fine!!'

'So what made you think he wasn't?' asked Mum.

'Georgina!' cried Bryony. 'She deliberately let me think that Red had wandered off and she'd *let* him!'

'On a day when anything might have happened to him,' added Emma.

'*What?*' cried Grandpa. 'What a rotten trick! Even for Georgina!'

'But, Bryony,' said Mum, 'if you think about it, it didn't make sense, did it? I mean, why *would*

199

Georgina let Red stray away when that boy that you told me about yesterday was just about to come and buy him?'

'I know!' Bryony felt so foolish now. 'I should have worked it out! It was just ... well, the way she *said* it, Mum. The way she says everything! She just gets me so angry and confused I don't think straight!'

'She messes with people's heads,' added Josh.

'Yes – she does, Mrs May,' Emma nodded.

'She's really, really mean!' cried Will crossly.

Grandpa went off to find Mr Lawrence and tell him that his children were safe. While he did, Bryony's mum walked them all back to Gardener's Cottage.

As they waited for Emma's dad, Emma got Bryony some cooled boiled water and sat beside her as she cleaned her cut.

'Em, I'm really sorry,' Bryony said. 'For – well – everything.'

'Don't be,' replied Emma. 'I know what Georgina's like, remember!'

Just then, Emma's dad rushed in.

'Thank goodness!' he cried, hugging Emma and Will. 'You're safe!'

He thanked Bryony's mum for finding them.

'Well, we sort of found each other,' she replied.

'Right, then,' Grandpa nodded. 'I think we'd best be off!'

Bryony popped a plaster onto her cut and then she and Emma gave each other a hug.

'Thanks again,' Bryony whispered.

'No worries,' smiled Emma. 'That's what best friends are for.' And after everything they'd been through they'd probably be best friends for life!

Mr Lawrence waved them off, then went back in to light a fire.

'Come on, then,' said Mum. 'Let's get you two home for tea, and Grandpa too.'

They were just about to head out through the back gate when Bryony heard it floating on the breeze. The sad *tap, tap, tap*, of a little hoof.

'Red!' she cried. 'He's *calling* me. Calling to say goodbye!' And turning, Bryony ran to him. She ran and never looked back. This time she was determined – *nothing* was going to stop her . . .

And there he was! Her beautiful Red, peeping out of his stable door. His eyes twinkled when he saw Bryony and his chocolate-coloured ears

201

pricked up. Then throwing back his head, Bryony's heart melted as he let out an excited little whinny.

'Oh, Red!' cried Bryony, throwing her arms round his neck. 'I'm so sorry I let you down. I wanted to keep you so much! And *no one* will love you like I do. Please, Red, never forget that, and be happy.'

Through a blur of tears Bryony saw Mum, Josh and Grandpa appear. They knew how much Bryony *wanted* Red, but now they saw how much she *needed* him too. And the little pony seemed to need Bryony back.

No one heard the footsteps until it was too late. Then suddenly the yard was filled with people.

'Oh . . .?' Arabella Brook looked very shocked. And there by her side was Georgina. Behind them stood Jonathan with his parents.

Georgina stepped forward.

'Get *off* my land!' She was looking right at Bryony. Bryony felt her cheeks burn at being caught saying a tearful goodbye.

'Well, what are you *waiting* for?' Georgina's eyes flashed. 'It's not like the stupid pony's going to miss *you*!'

'Georgina!' Bella looked suddenly mortified. 'Why on earth are you talking to Bryony like this?'

As Bryony had suspected, Bella had no idea what her daughter was *really* like.

'At least I don't blackmail people,' Bryony retorted. 'And make them lie, Georgina!'

Bryony turned to Bella.

'I'm sorry, Mrs Brook, but the truth is,' she said, 'Georgina has never loved that pony. She never even gave him a *name*. And she forced me to lie to my mother for just a few small moments alone with Red. Yes, *Red* is his name. *I* gave it to him when Georgina called him nothing . . .'

Bella gaped as the dreadful truth about her daughter finally dawned on her.

'Right!' Georgina rounded on Jonathan. 'Do you want this dumb pony or not?'

'Georgina!!' Bella looked close to tears and Jonathan's parents looked outraged. Tutting, they ushered their son past Georgina.

'Hey, where are you *going*?!' Georgina roared after them.

'To find a pony that's been better looked after!' frowned Jonathan's dad.

Bryony's mum put her arm around her. 'It's time for us to go too.'

'But *Red* . . .' sobbed Bryony under her breath.

'Come on, pumpkin,' Grandpa whispered. 'Let's get you home and dry.' And they left Bella to deal with her daughter, alone.

*

That night, as Bryony lay awake in bed, Grandpa brought her in a mug of cocoa.

'Just wanted to see you're okay?' he said. 'Before I head home, you know.'

'I just love Red so much,' Bryony whispered.

'I know,' Grandpa nodded. 'And Red knows it too. Sometimes,' he said, 'the most difficult things have a way of working out right.'

'I *wish* . . .' whispered Bryony, trying hard *not* to in case she was hurt again.

'Night, Gramps,' she said.

'Aye,' replied Grandpa. 'Night-night.'

Chapter 15

'But, Grandpa, where are we going?' asked Bryony.

'You'll see!' Grandpa nodded back. 'There's a problem that needs *sorting* and you're the only one who can do it!'

It was Monday afternoon and Bryony had spent the whole day thinking about Red. So what if *Jonathan* didn't buy him? Someone else was bound to fall in love with him soon ...

They rounded the corner into the main street. Miss Pigeon was out sweeping the shop's step.

'Well, if it isn't young Bryony,' she smiled. 'You and Emma got second in fête flowers!'

'I know,' replied Bryony. Though that seemed such a long time ago ...

'I *know* you know!' Miss Pigeon now nodded. 'As I can read the *future*, you see.'

'Yes, we know that too!' Grandpa chuckled softly.

'And *I* won the jam and 'er *didn't*!' went on Miss Pigeon, nodding in the direction of Miss Parsley's pink house. 'But then 'er went and *whacked* me with this dirty great *crow*!'

Miss Pigeon tutted. 'Where you off to, then?'

'I'd have thought you'd *know* that!' Grandpa grinned.

'Huh! Just checking!' Miss Pigeon puffed. 'Had *so* many visions today, I have – don't know if I'm coming or going! Ooooh!' she cried. 'And 'ere come a couple more!'

She closed her eyes for a moment, concentrating hard whilst sucking on her vision-enhancing liquorice-stick.

'Come on, then!' puffed Miss Pigeon, jiggling her head round a bit as if a few were slightly wedged. But then all of a sudden – out they came . . .

'I see a *hill*, I see a *car*, I see—'

'*Seagull poo on your step?*' asked Grandpa as the seagull it belonged to flapped away.

'You WHAT?!' Miss Pigeon's blue eyes suddenly opened. The seagull had got her *slippers* too . . .

'Grr, now I shall have to sponge down me pompoms!' she ranted.

Leaving her to it, Grandpa waved goodbye, continuing along the street with Bryony. 'Pity she hadn't seen *that* one coming!' he grinned.

Grandpa seemed really happy today.

'Hmm . . .' said Bryony as they climbed the hill together. 'Hey, Miss Pigeon just saw a *hill*, didn't she? I wonder, well – if it was *this* one?'

Grandpa snorted. But Bryony also then remembered that at the fête, in her fortune-telling tent, Miss Pigeon had foreseen *water* too. And Sunday's storm had most definitely been wet!

They continued up the hill and along the headland jutting out into the sea.

'Grandpa, doesn't this lead to Seaview Stables?' asked Bryony. Grandpa was now striding on ahead. Bryony had seen the stables from down on the beach but never actually visited, despite having been invited by Abi.

Bryony *had* thought of, maybe, popping up there with Red, but Georgina had got better, of course,

and taken Red back. And going there *without* him would have been way too hard.

Bryony sighed. Not *nearly* as hard as it felt right now, though, trying to avoid seeing ponies going in, their riders all chatting happily. After saying goodbye to Red yesterday it was all so sad.

Grandpa *usually*, thought Bryony, knew exactly what to do when she needed cheering up. But *this* certainly *wasn't* it!

'Bryony, hi!' It was Hari who rode the Welsh Connemara cross. She was with Alice and Finn. Hari said they were heading to the stables for their riding lesson, and *would* stop to talk but they were late.

'No worries,' said Bryony. 'You go on. We'll catch up another time!'

'They looked nice,' said Grandpa when they'd gone. But Bryony was relieved they hadn't stopped for a chat as she couldn't have coped with them asking after Red. Not today!

No sooner had they gone, though, than Grandpa said to Bryony, 'We'd better get going too!'

Bryony didn't understand. They hadn't *been* anywhere yet. But Grandpa started walking and Bryony followed.

'Hang on!' called Bryony. 'Grandpa – wait!' *He* was heading into the stables too!

'Grandpa!' she gasped, following him across the busy yard. She tried to ignore the children mucking out their ponies, or grooming them, or tacking them up. But the clatter of hooves as ponies came and went, and the sound of people (and ponies!) calling, soon blended into a chorus of happy chaos reminding Bryony so much of her old riding stables back in the city.

'Grandpa, *wait!*' Bryony cried. This was all so difficult! 'We're not meant to be here. I—'

'Don't worry.' Grandpa patted her arm. 'They're *expecting* you, pumpkin, you see?'

'Expecting me, but—'

'Nearly there now!' smiled Grandpa. 'Come on!'

He rounded a corner and Bryony followed. Then suddenly her heart skipped a beat. She closed her eyes. She was imagining it. She opened them again. No – she wasn't! For there, in a stable, peeping out at her was ... Red!

'Grandpa, how ...?' Bryony stopped in her tracks. 'Has someone *bought* him? Who?'

'You.'

'Me?!'

'Why, yes!'

Grandpa nodded. 'Surprise!!' he cried. And Red was now whinnying excitedly.

Then above his stable door Bryony saw . . .

RED

Owner: Miss Bryony Elizabeth May

Bryony had to read it several times before she could actually *believe* it. The paint on the sign was glistening, still not quite dry.

'He's ... *mine?*' Bryony could hardly get the word out.

'*All* yours!' Grandpa beamed.

'But, Grandpa,' gasped Bryony. 'I didn't have enough money!'

'I helped you, just a little,' Grandpa nodded.

'But, Grandpa – *you* don't have the money either!'

Then Bryony saw Grandpa's old driving gloves peeping out of his jacket pocket.

'G-Grandpa, you *didn't* . . .'

'Sell *Matilde?*' Grandpa answered. 'Why, yes!'

Bryony gasped. 'But you *love* that old car!'

'Not as much as I love you. Or Red.'

'But *when* did you sell it?' Bryony asked. And suddenly . . .

'*Car*,' Bryony gasped. *Miss Pigeon had seen a CAR too!*

'I decided,' said Grandpa, 'when I left you last night, that my old MG was a *finished* project and I needed a new project to begin. So I sold the car to a pal from the car show, first thing this morning!'

Grandpa looked genuinely happy. And Bryony found herself smiling back.

'Well, what are you waiting for?' Grandpa chuckled. 'Aren't you going to hug your new pony?'

With that, Bryony raced to the stable door and threw her arms around Red.

'Oh, Red!' she cried, smelling his delicious smell. 'Now that I've got you, I'm *never* going to let you go!'

And Red gave a happy nicker, like he was cheering, 'Yippee!'

'And so say all of us!' Grandpa said with a smile.

Then who should appear but Emma. 'Hi,

Bryony!' And Josh, Will and Mum were with her too.

'Wow!' said Emma. 'Red looks like he's *smiling*.'

'I know!' beamed Bryony. 'Thanks to you all!'

'And *you*,' Emma nodded. 'What a team!'

'Oh, but, Grandpa!' gasped Bryony. 'You said there was a *problem* that only *I* could sort out?'

'Ah, don't go looking so worried!' said Grandpa. 'The thing is, the money from the car bought Red.'

'After LOTS of persuading from Grandpa,' chipped in Mum. 'Bella was totally fine about it but Georgina *really* kicked off. In the end that's what made Bella sell him to you. To teach her daughter that she can't always have her way!'

'Anyway,' smiled Grandpa, 'where *you* come in, Bryony, is making sure that Red can *stay* here.'

He explained that he couldn't afford full livery for Red.

'That means . . .' said Grandpa.

'I know!' Bryony nodded. 'It means I have to be here every day mucking him out. And exercising him, and taking him out on hacks.'

Bryony smiled. 'That's fine by me! I wouldn't

have it *any* other way! With good ponies come great responsibilities, I know that.'

'There you go,' Grandpa beamed. 'Problem sorted!'

Mum also added that part of the deal was that sometimes other children were allowed to ride Red too when they came to Seaview Stables for their lessons.

'No problem!' smiled Bryony. 'Red knows that I'll always be there for him.' And after almost losing him *for ever* – sharing him a bit was the least of her worries now.

Josh offered to help Bryony muck out Red any time she wanted.

'Me too!' said Emma.

'Me three!' piped up Will. 'I love shovelling!'

'And we'll watch you in competitions,' said Emma. 'Those – what are they called? Like *pyjamas* ...?'

'Gymkhanas!' giggled Bryony. 'Brilliant! Thanks, Em, I'll be doing lots of those – i–if Red wants to.'

At this, Red nodded his head and blew what sounded like a big happy raspberry.

'I think that means: *Yes!*' Bryony laughed.

She couldn't help thinking that Georgina would want her own back. But that was in the *future* and this was now.

And Miss Pigeon, thought Bryony, was a genius!

Author's Note

When I was little, my brother (who was a lot older than me) had a dog called Prince. I have vague memories of how soft and cuddly Prince was. But Prince died when I was really young and after that I was told we couldn't have another dog, even though I always longed for one.

I was allowed to keep the goldfish that I won in fairgrounds. They used to come in bags, poor things. I used to talk to them and watch them swimming round, but obviously you can't cuddle a goldfish . . .

I was then allowed a budgie and I used to let him out to fly around the front room. He was called Joey and was green and swore a bit, which was embarrassing when guests came. I can't remember who taught him the swear words. He said other, much better words too, like: 'Hello!' and: 'Who's a pretty boy, then?'. Still though, Joey wasn't all that cuddly, you know?

Then one day, when I was walking home from the shops, a 'stray' kitten just appeared from nowhere and followed me home. (I'd like to *think* that she was a stray anyway . . .)

At first my mother said we couldn't keep her. But I was tenacious, which is a posh way of saying a right nag, and eventually my mother caved in. So – hooray! – the tortoiseshell kitten became mine and I called her Tibby.

From then on, Tibby was cuddled *so much* (and often wheeled round in my doll's pram). She listened when I was sad, purred when I was happy and occasionally swiped me when she'd had enough of the doll's pram.

Tibby had a long and very contented life. She became my mother's companion when I finally left home to go to college. Pets understand when words fall short. They have instinct, and if you treat them well, they'll love you unconditionally.

Since Tibby, I've had *many* more pets, all different and all very special. I've never had a pony. Not yet anyway. But, who knows, maybe one day . . .

Tracey Corderoy